LOST HORSES

LOST HORSES

– Seven Stories –

Mark Saha

The author may be reached for inquiries about rights and permissions at sahamark735@gmail.com

Sincere thanks to Liz Villasenor for suggesting the title, and to George Crowder for many valuable comments on the manuscript.

"The Blind Horse" originally appeared in Write Away, published by Santa Monica Public Library.

Chelsea Press
Los Angeles, CA

First Edition, 2019

ISBN: 9780997935820 (paperback)
ISBN 9780997935837 (e-book)
Library of Congress Control Number: 2018961036

Printed in the United States of America

Book Cover Design by ebooklaunch.com
Editing and Page Layout by Polgarus Studio
Chelsea Press logo by Luis Contreras

For Brigitta, with love

Logic can prove nothing of interest to the human heart.

— Bertrand Russell

CONTENTS

THE BLIND HORSE

When my grandfather died in the 1950s, Dad inherited a modest 130-acre cotton farm near Sealy, about fifty miles from where we lived in Houston. There was a small but comfortable farmhouse on the property, a windmill and water tank, electricity for lighting and refrigeration, but no telephone. What I liked best was the eight-acre pond Grandpa had created many years back by damming the creek that crossed our property.

The lake, as I called it, was a good ten feet deep where the dam sat above the old creek bed, but quickly shallowed out as the water moved into open pasture. Grandpa had stocked it with perch and bass and the fishing was very good. By chance it was also located under a major bird migration route and attracted a lot of ducks headed south for the winter. During hunting season you could pretty much bag as many as you could eat.

Dad learned that the tenant who lived rent-free on the

place worked a full time job in town and had not put in more than a few rows of cotton the past several years. What little he planted was overgrown with Johnson grass, which so choked the cotton that its sickly bolls were scarcely worth picking even by hand. Our share of the crop did not even meet property taxes on the farm, which Dad had to pay with earnings from his grocery and butcher shop in Houston.

He evicted the tenant and looked around for a more serious cotton farmer. We went through three or four in about as many years. Most had wives and children, and were eager to live on the place rent-free, but upon moving in found work in town. The windmill was rusted and in disrepair, the house needed painting, and none of the tenants made a significant effort to put a decent crop in the ground.

Because Dad's tenants spent so much time in town, poachers began sneaking onto the property to hunt and fish. The lakeshore became littered with beer cans and whiskey bottles, and one time Dad came across a pair of panties flung high into a tree. He was discouraged to find his inheritance little more than a property tax expense, but was reluctant to sell land that had been left to him by his father.

It occurred to him we could probably manage fifty or so head of cattle there to stock his butcher shop or sell at the cattle auction in Sealy. He evicted the latest tenant and went out of cotton farming. We repainted the farmhouse and repaired the windmill. He bought fifty head of red Herefords, and we put in a weather shelter and water trough for them.

I thought we were going to need horses to work cattle and had been excited about rounding them up on horseback. Dad put that idea right out of my head. "The day of the horse is dead and gone," he told me. "Anytime you see a man on a horse, you're looking at somebody who is losing money." He said feeding and caring for them would put us in a financial hole. If we needed to move cattle from one pasture to another, he would drive the pickup with me standing on the running board to shout and wave at them. If any drifted into the thick huisache brush at the far end of our property, we would go in on foot and chase them out with sticks.

I was about eleven or twelve then, and we drove out from Houston on weekends to work the cattle. Chores included buying bales of sorghum in Sealy and storing them in the weather shelter for the cows. Another regular task was checking the electric fences that separated grazing pastures to make sure they were operating properly. We were constantly on the lookout for sick cows, and ran them into the corral where we could look after them. What I liked most was going to the cattle auction in Sealy; I liked loading and hauling a cow or calf, and watching buyers bid on it in the auction pen. When there wasn't anything else for me to do, I was allowed to go rabbit hunting or fishing at the lake.

Johnny Wexler owned the property adjacent to ours and had watched with curiosity as my father turned the cotton farm into a cattle operation. One day he walked over to talk to us. Johnny had lost interest in farming after his wife left him and was looking for a way to make money off his own place without having to work. He had spoken to a couple of young horsemen who had experience working summer camps for the Boy Scouts, and they were willing to run a camp for city kids on his property if he would buy a couple dozen horses for trail rides. Johnny offered to pay us for permission to take boys and girls on horseback rides to our lake; they would fish, build campfires, and spend the night. He promised everything would be carefully supervised and any trash would be cleaned up after breaking camp. Dad told him to his face that he was a fool to invest good money in two dozen horses, but agreed to negotiate permission for the trail rides if that was what he decided.

We were working cattle a couple weeks later when Johnny invited us to come see his horses. They were amiable enough, an older-looking assortment of sleepy-eyed bay or chestnut mares and geldings safe for children. He did not know anything about horses, but somebody tipped him off to a rancher who let him have all twenty-seven of these for three thousand dollars.

Johnny boasted the rancher liked him so much that he had thrown in an old blind horse he did not want. The flea-bitten gray gelding did not have a name so far as I knew, and everybody just called it the blind horse. Dad did not see the sense of accepting a horse that wasn't good for anything because he would have to feed and care for it same as the others. But Johnny looked more proud of his free horse than the rest put together, and was offended when Dad suggested the rancher had tricked him to get rid of it.

Over the following summer, when Dad and I were working cattle, we often saw Johnny's camp counselors leading kids on horseback expeditions to our lake. After they broke camp and left in the morning, we would walk over and inspect the grounds. They always cleaned up before going, and we received a check from Johnny each month. Dad was starting to like the arrangement, but was also becoming aggravated about the blind horse.

Johnny allowed it to roam freely on his own property, but it could tell when the other horses were leaving for a trail ride on ours. Though blind as a bat, it had learned to slip out the gate with them. Whenever we came out from Houston to work cattle, it was usually wandering loose somewhere on our pastures. I didn't see where it was doing any harm or eating much grass to speak of. And somebody always came to get it soon as Dad complained. But next time we'd come out to work cattle, there the blind horse would be, grazing on our land. My father became aggravated to the point where, if he did not see it on our property, he would go looking for it.

Sometimes Dad went to the farm alone, and one

evening over dinner he told me and Mom what had happened. "Do you know where I found that bugger today? He was way over on the other side of the lake in the huisache. That brush is so thick a man can hardly walk through it. What business did he think he had over there?" Dad must have wasted at least a couple of hours of daylight looking for him.

One day we were breaking open sorghum bales for cattle when Johnny showed up with a halter to fetch the blind horse. Dad called him over and made a proposition.

"Johnny, have you ever tasted horse meat?"

"Don't know anything about the stuff."

"I hear it's a real delicacy in France. People pay big money for it in Europe. You have to be well-to-do over there to walk into a restaurant and order a horse steak."

Johnny admitted he had never been to France.

"Why don't you let me butcher that bugger," Dad offered. "Let's divide him up. I bet he'll last us a year."

Johnny turned red in the face. "Nobody is going to eat that horse while I'm alive, James!" he shouted. "No sir! I don't care what they do in France!"

"That bugger's not worth a thin dime," Dad told him. "You're losing money on him."

"Well, he's not bothering anybody," Johnny huffed. He slipped a halter on the animal and led it back to his property.

That fall a Category 3 hurricane came ashore near

Galveston. It quickly broke up after landfall, but carried soaking rains deep inland. The street flooded up to our porch step in Houston, and Dad worried about property damage on the farm. He was pretty sure the shallow end of the lake had flooded the pasture where we left the cattle, and hoped they had retreated to higher ground around the farmhouse. We were also worried about water spilling over the dam and causing it to fail, sending a wall of water from our property toward the state highway.

We waited a couple days after the rains passed to let the water subside before attempting to reach the farm. Soon as we pulled off the highway onto the gravel-top county road to our place, we saw ditches filled with water almost to road level. That was a bad sign. Sure enough, we arrived to find much of the farm under several inches of water. The narrow, raised rutted road to the house was still above water but looked muddy and slick.

Dad studied the situation and estimated we could make it if he crept forward in low gear. I was wide-eyed the whole way. He crossed several deep potholes, and we navigated a stretch where water had washed out the road and was spilling into pasture on the far side. Eventually we pulled onto high ground around the house.

The cattle had sheltered there as we hoped, and we broke open several sorghum bales for them to eat. Then we pulled on rubber boots and made our way across pasture to the dam. The water was high but not spilling over, so we knew it was going to hold. After sloshing around the property a few hours and finding no serious damage, my father announced that we might as well go home. There was no point in spending the night because we could not do much until the water subsided, and he wanted to leave before dark.

Dad was more confident about the road this time but crept forward in low gear anyway. We had not gone very far when we came upon the blind horse. He was standing in the middle of the road with his backside toward us.

"Look at that," Dad said. "There's that bugger! I wondered where he went. What does he think he's doing?"

"He can't see anything," I reminded Dad. Probably he had been splashing through flooded pasture and blundered upon the high ground of the road. The horse stood there calmly as if in idle thought. It did not look like he intended to move anytime soon.

"Well, he doesn't have any business there." Dad did not want to startle him so he tapped the horn lightly a couple times. The horse acted like it was deaf as well as blind.

"I don't think he's going anywhere now," I said. "He's found himself a dry spot."

Dad was getting impatient. "Come on, mister. I've got a cold beer waiting for me at home." He pressed the horn louder, and when that did not work, gave it a long hard blast. The old flea-bitten gray horse didn't flinch. He must have heard us this time, but was not about to return to the flooded pasture.

"You have to move it, buster," Dad said. He eased his foot from the clutch, and the truck crept forward to tap the gelding gently on the behind.

WHAM! That horse ripped loose with a kick that rocked the truck from front to back. We rattled in the cab like a pair of dice in a dice cup. When we came to our senses the horse was still standing there, and we heard water splashing to the ground. We slid out of the cab and looked under the truck. The radiator was kicked in and split, emptying the last of its water onto the ground.

Dad got back to his feet and stared at the horse. It stood firm on dry ground and was not going anywhere. "Look at him! That thing is as stubborn as he is blind, you know it?" Dad could get pretty aggravated about stuff but I hardly ever saw him lose his temper. "Well, that's it then," he sighed, accepting the new situation with a shake of his head. "That bugger broke us down."

We were not going anywhere without a radiator. The nearest mechanic was at the Riverside Café about a dozen miles back, where the state highway crossed the Brazos River.

"I'm an old man, son," he told me. "It looks like you have to go find us a tow truck." He settled into the cab and found an unfinished sandwich in the glove compartment.

It was five miles of county road just to reach the highway.

I always liked horses and never saw where this one was doing any harm grazing in our pastures. But once I realized how far it was to the river on foot, I had to admit he could be aggravating.

"Darned blind horse!" I told myself, kicking sprays of gravel ahead of me the whole way.

THE GETAWAY OF EDDIE LEE JESSUP

Edgar Lee Jessup murdered his wife in the spring of 1878. She had been fetching a bucket of water when he clipped her from behind with an ax handle. Somebody found her by the water pump behind their house a couple of days later. By that time Jessup had gathered his weapons and ammunition, packed his saddlebags, and set out for parts unknown.

Eddie Jessup was a familiar figure to Dunsmuir County Sheriff Deputy Bob Holloway at Cleburne. Bob lived with his wife Dorothea in the residential quarters behind the jailhouse. Jessup had spent the night in one of his cells on several occasions for public drunkenness or reckless discharge of firearms. The telegraph company had let him go on account of his drinking, and Bob had been pretty sure Eddie was abusing his wife. He wished he had found opportunity to shoot the bastard before it had come to this. Now Dorothea was upset because her husband was going to be heading out with a posse to who-knows-where for God-knows-how-long.

Bob hated soliciting married men for pursuit duty because they had families to look after. However, most were in their forties or fifties, when he believed men to be more mature and reliable, and some even had trail experience. Reluctantly, he put the tap on millinery shop owner Cullen Aleshire, farrier Owen Blewitt, horse rancher Jeff Haskell, and Captain Jack Schoepff, a carpenter who had held that rank in the war. Jack was a veteran of the Red River campaign in Louisiana that had prevented a Union invasion of Texas, and was the most experienced of the bunch, including the sheriff.

Bob wanted one more fellow but hesitated to ask barber shop owner Hugh Thermin because his wife had just given birth. He also discouraged young Nathan Osterhaus, who was pestering him in the worst way, but had only turned seventeen last week. Nate would be the sole unmarried member of the hunt, but to Bob's mind that was his only virtue. It was Bob's experience that while kids of that age were enthusiastic, they often proved more of a hazard to themselves and the posse than to the fugitive.

The boy would not leave him alone. Nate was an only child whose father had been killed in the war and who still lived with his deeply religious mother. He was desperate to escape the boredom of living with his mother and working as a hardware store clerk.

"I own a sound horse and a good rifle, and I'm a dead shot," he said. "I want to see places and learn things." He was a nice enough looking kid; tall with blue eyes and brown curly hair, and bursting with enthusiasm. He would be by far the greenest of the bunch.

Bob decided to leave Hugh Thermin behind to look after his wife, but did not feel he could deputize a kid of barely seventeen without at least saying something to his mother. He stopped by the Osterhaus residence for her thoughts on the matter, and to his surprise found she was delighted.

"I believe God put us on this earth for one purpose only, and that is to do His will," she said. "It's a terrible thing what happened to that woman. Anybody who helps bring Eddie Jessup to justice is serving God."

"Alice, you need to appreciate we're talking about a manhunt. This could end in a shoot-out. We'll be sleeping on open prairie where there's snakes and wild animals."

"It's not snakes and animals I'm worried about," she said. "It's these girls right here in Cleburne that will send that boy straight to hell. He's shot up like a weed this past year, and with those blue eyes and curly hair, they can't keep their eyes off him. I worry every day some mother is going to knock on my door to say my son put her daughter with child. He's at a real bad age, and I don't know how much longer I can hold them off. I hope you do take him out onto the prairie, and keep him there as long as you need to accomplish God's will. I'll have a little peace of mind for once, and can sleep nights knowing he's someplace the town girls can't get him."

When Bob told Hugh Thermin's wife that he had found a rifle and saddle to replace her husband, she threw her arms around him and burst into tears of gratitude. "Dottie, it looks like the menfolks in Cleburne will be able to get a haircut and shave while I'm gone this time," he said, laughing.

That night Bob gathered the posse in his office to deputize them. Young Nate brought his repeating rifle to show everybody and bragged about his ability to hit tin cans. Captain Schoepff ordered him to put the damn thing away and not pull it from its boot again until he had to use it. Bob swore in each man in turn, and each was given a tin star to pin on his shirt.

"Jessup is armed to the teeth and likely liquored up," Bob said. "Expect one hell of a scrap when we run the bastard to ground. I want everybody to go home and pack, say your farewells to family, and get a good night's sleep. We'll meet back here at daybreak."

He dismissed the posse but asked Schoepff to stay behind to discuss something.

"Bob, what in the world did you have on your mind besides your hat when you swore in that Osterhaus kid?" Schoepff said.

"You must have commanded a lot of boys his age during the war, Jack."

"I sure did. That's why I don't like it."

"Anyway, I have some ideas about this manhunt I want to run past you."

"You need to bring me up to date, first," Schoepff said. "Where do we stand on this thing?"

"Dorothea's been at the telegraph office sending alerts all down the wire. So far nobody's seen him."

"Eddie Lee has a two day start on us, and we don't even know which direction he went?"

"Jack, I can't begin to tell you how much I want this bastard."

"Well, it doesn't look to me like we have one whole hell of a lot to work with."

"I believe we need to be scientific about this," Bob said. "Let me show you something."

They stepped over to the office wall map of Dunsmuir and adjacent counties.

"We're living in modern times," Bob said. "The railroad is replacing the horse for commerce and transport, and the telegraph wire for communication. Our man knows this, and he knows that's what is going to trip him up. I believe Jessup intends to avoid our communication lines by sticking to open country on horseback."

He glanced at Jack for comment. The captain waited for him to elaborate.

"Now, with a sound horse on good roads, I estimate he can make about forty miles a day," Bob said. "He would be a fool not to stay on the best roads. That ought to put him eighty to a hundred miles out of Cleburne somewhere along here." He made a circular motion with his finger to trace a circumference around Cleburne. "We've got mountains to the west, so that leaves just three good roads where he can make that kind of time."

Schoepff picked up on Bob's thinking, pointing to roads north, east, and south from town where they crossed the circle Bob had traced with his finger.

"Now look at the telegraph wires," Bob said. "I believe they are the key to the puzzle."

"You said Dorothea didn't hear anything from them."

Bob nodded. "Eddie worked for the telegraph company and knows the lines real good. He intends to stay the hell away from them, because that's where people will be on the alert. This tells me he's not headed east. See how the wire density gets thicker the farther east you go? It's a real rat's nest back there."

"I believe that's called the multilateral oligopoly," Schoepff said.

Bob paused a moment, but decided not to ask the captain to elaborate. "Anyway, he's not going there." Bob's finger drifted to the road south of town. "Now this takes him to the railroad trunk line to San Francisco. Look at all those spur lines connecting towns to it. He won't go anywhere near them, either."

Schoepff was studying the remaining road. "Cleburne is the terminal of the telegraph feed line from the main wire that follows the railroad. If he went north, he's left the railroad and telegraph behind."

"Which is why Dorothea isn't getting any word of him on the wire. At forty miles a day, he must be right about here," Bob said, moving his finger to a spot between Bottle and Cleburne. "He'll reach Bottle sometime late tomorrow. Another day and a half puts him at Bottle's Pass. Once through there, he's looking at nothing but daylight."

Schoepff was following this, but did not look happy about it.

"I'm confident he's headed for California," Bob said. "Once he's past those mountains, pretty much the only telegraph lines west follow the railroads. If he stays clear of them, he's got a clean shot to the Pacific and nobody is ever going to see him again."

Schoepff studied the map for a flaw in the sheriff's thinking but could find none. "I hate to admit this, but it looks to me like he's got us whupped."

"I'm glad you said that, Jack," Bob said. "You just confirmed my thinking. I wanted to make sure I figured this right."

"I must have missed something then, if you see a solution to this."

"Well, I found this feed wire west of the mountains that runs up from the railroad to Fedora. Fellow name of Arlan Briscoe is sheriff there. Dorothea wired him yesterday. Fedora is less than a two-day ride to the egress of Bottle's Pass. Arlan says he can throw a posse across there before we reach Bottle. If we stay hot on Jessup from this end, and Arlan blocks the egress, I don't see how that asswipe has anyplace left to go."

Schoepff looked at Fedora on the map. "Well goddamn, Bob," he said. "I believe I need to buy you a drink."

"We can talk about that once we close this deal," Bob said. "It's still a tight game we're running. I need you to stay on top of my thinking. We don't want to blunder this opportunity away somehow."

"There's a lot can go wrong in the field, but I'd say this looks as close to a lock as a man can expect in this life," Schoepff said.

The posse gathered outside the sheriff's office shortly before dawn. They were veteran deputies, grimly silent and professional, anticipating the hard day ahead. Nate arrived on a young roan gelding, easily the fastest horse of the lot. He was unable to contain his excitement and rode a couple of circles around the others. Then he put his horse in a little spin while waving his rifle in the air and hooting loudly. Schoepff walked his horse alongside the boy and talked him down, impressing upon him the seriousness of the business at hand. Nate apologized and promised to behave. Bob did not say anything, but made up his mind on the spot that no way in hell did he want this kid mixed up in a shoot-out. He resolved to get shed of young Osterhaus at the first opportunity.

The posse headed north out of Cleburne at daybreak, spent one night on the prairie under the stars, and rode into Bottle shortly after dark on the second day. Everybody was hot and tired, so Bob treated them to a dinner at the hotel and rooms for the night at the county's expense. While the men bathed and ate, he made enquiries around town and spoke with the local constable. He was not happy about what he learned. He went back to the hotel, but the posse had finished eating and had left. He found them in a saloon teaching Nate how to knock back a shot.

"Boys, order me the strongest drink in the house," Bob said. "We need to sit and talk."

They moved to a table along the far wall with their drinks. Bob said several people in Bottle had encountered Jessup and identified his photograph. The rascal was stinking drunk and threw a whiskey bottle at one of them. Jessup wanted to pass out in the hotel and sleep for a week, but the clerk refused to book him a room. When Jessup became belligerent the constable was called and escorted him out of town. Now came the bad part. The constable told Bob that Jessup had not taken the road west to Bottle's Pass, but had instead continued north.

Everybody fell silent and thought about this.

"That makes no sense at all," said Jeff Haskell, who was familiar with the country up there. "He's headed into the barrens. It's nothing but hilly scrub with no settlements for miles. He won't make twenty miles a day in that country and there's no place to go anyway. I'd say he's lost his mind."

"He's crazy like a snake," Bob said. "Jessup knows the wires and figured we'd telegraph Fedora to have them cover the pass. The constable tells me there's an unblazed crossing north of here called Dug's Gap. Not many people know about it because it won't take wagons, and he'll need a good day and a half on horseback. But Jessup's going to punch through there and be clear of the wires with a clean shot to California."

They sat in silence a moment. "I didn't come all this way for nothing," Owen Blewitt said.

"I don't like it either, Owen," Bob said. "But it looks to me like the bastard's outsmarted us."

Schoepff spoke up. "We need to send somebody back to Cleburne to shoot a wire to Fedora. Have them dispatch a rider to Arlan's posse and instruct them to proceed to Dug's Gap."

Bob shook his head. "It's two days to Cleburne, and then Fedora would have to send a rider to catch Arlan. Jessup will be gone by then."

Again there was silence. Everyone pondered the conundrum.

"Bob, I know how you can put a telegram in Fedora by tomorrow afternoon at three o'clock," Cullen Aleshire said.

Bob looked at him with cautious interest. "How do you figure that, Cullen?"

"My wife is from a little place called McCook. It's about ten hours due east of here if you know how to cross the river. This just occurred to me. McCook is the terminal of a telegraph feed wire from the rail spur in Jasper."

He had everybody's attention. "Cullen, are you sure about this?" Bob asked.

"I know McCook really well, but didn't even think about the telegraph until now."

"Tell me about the river," Bob said.

"Well, I wouldn't waste time looking for a ford this time of year. There's a fellow named Rufus Foster runs a little unlicensed horse-and-wagon ferry you need to find. He charges a dollar but it's worth it. I'd say it's about seven hours to the ferry. Once over the river, another three hours will put you in McCook."

"If I send somebody at daybreak, he can be in McCook by three o'clock?"

"That's what I'm telling you."

Bob got up and walked to the hotel next door, asked the desk clerk for stationary, and wrote a communication instructing the Fedora sheriff's office to dispatch a rider to Arlan's posse and have them proceed to Dug's Gap.

He returned to the tavern and slapped a silver dollar on the table in front of Nate. Then he slid the envelope with the communication to the boy.

"Son, you've had enough to drink tonight," he said. "Go get some sleep. You're heading out at first light for McCook."

"The hell you say! I volunteered for a damn manhunt. I'm not your messenger boy."

"Maybe somebody forgot to explain this part. You are deputized, you are under oath, and you take orders from me. Your sorry ass is going to McCook and delivering this to the telegraph office. Now finish that drink and go to bed."

Nate stared at the envelope and silver dollar. "Are you going to wait for me?"

"Hell, no. We'll be moving out for Dug's Gap. There's no way you can catch up to us. Once you deliver this message, you are discharged from duty. Go on back home to Cleburne."

The boy looked devastated.

"Don't worry, son," Owen said. "I'll put an extra bullet in Jessup for you, and tell you all about it when we get back."

"Say, with any luck we might even catch him asleep in camp," Jeff Haskell said. "We'll sneak up and unload on him in his blanket."

Everybody laughed. Owen spoke up again. "Then we'll celebrate here a few days before going home. It's going to be one hell of a party!"

"Don't worry, Nate," Jeff said, reaching over to slap him on the back. "We'll tell you all about it when we get back."

"Leave the kid alone," Schoepff said. "This is his first posse and he's doing fine."

"They're just messing with you, son," Bob said. "Every man at this table is depending on you."

"Yes sir, Sheriff," the boy said reluctantly. "I'll do my duty."

He finished his drink, swept up the envelope and silver dollar, and left for the hotel.

The posse set out for Dug's Gap at daybreak. Nate detached and headed east to McCook. He made good time, and a little before noon cleared a rise overlooking the river. Descending into the bottomland, he saw a dense copse of oak and cottonwood and lush grazing grass along the meandering banks. He'd been riding almost seven hours, and was tempted to allow his horse to water and graze while he took a nap in the cool shade of the trees. On another day he might have done so, but he was a deputized officer of the law dispatched on an important duty, and proceeded to search for the ferry.

Nate followed Cullen's directions and shortly came upon a modest living structure and a ferry dock on his side of the river. He was not much impressed with Cullen's idea of a ferry. It looked to be little more than a wooden raft made of scrap lumber beached on the far bank. There was a heavy-duty guide rope strung across the river between two telegraph poles, and ropes attached to each end of the raft had been tied to sliding brass rings on the guide rope. He also saw a couple of slender poles alongside the raft that were apparently used to propel it across the river.

It did not look much worth a dollar to him. He wondered if he might scout for a ford, but Cullen had said not to waste time with that. It occurred to him that maybe he could shit around with this old bastard, demand free transport as a lawman on duty, and keep the silver dollar Sheriff Holloway had given him for passage.

Nobody was in sight on the lazy afternoon. He was a half hour ahead of schedule, with McCook only another three hours on the far side, and no longer felt particularly hurried.

"Hello!" he shouted. Nobody answered. He dismounted the roan and tested the wooden dock railing. It was weathered and not very sturdy.

"Rufus Foster!" he shouted again.

"He's not here!" a girl's voice yelled back from the other side of the shack.

Nathan led his horse around the shack and discovered her on a scenic porch that overlooked the river. She was eighteen at most, barefoot and wearing only a simple cotton print dress, tipped back in a chair against the porch railing, drinking a beer from a stoneware bottle. There was a wooden tub of beer chilled in cold river water resting on the porch near her chair.

She took in the young lawman holding the reins of a trim roan gelding.

"Daddy went to town and I'm drinking all his beer," she said. She pulled another sip from the bottle.

Nate had not expected to stumble across somebody

like this on a manhunt, and froze up so bad that he was unable to speak. He had no experience with girls and was scared to death of them. His mother had never allowed him anywhere near them without supervision.

She saw the look on his face and figured he was not going to say anything. "You should unbridle that horse and let it graze a little," she said. "If you want, you can come sit on the porch and have a beer."

Nate believed if he drew himself up straight and spoke with authority, he might muster the courage to say something. "I'm a deputized officer of the law on a manhunt for a killer. I have an urgent communication for the telegraph office at McCook."

His bravado elicited the faint twitch of a smile. "Well, aren't you the one!" She finished the beer, tossed the bottle into the river, and tipped forward on the chair to pull another from the tub.

"Sheriff Holloway gave me a dollar for the ferry."

"I'm in charge while Daddy's away. You have to negotiate with me."

"When will he be back?"

"Sometimes he's gone several days."

"I see he left the damn ferry on the other side. What do we do about that?"

"I suppose somebody will have to swim over and fetch it."

"You don't have a rowboat or anything?"

"Daddy shot a hole in it."

"Well, that's a bitch."

She twisted the wire from the bottle, pulled the stopper with a corkscrew, and took a swallow. "The world's not going to end in the next ten minutes if you have a beer with me. Unbridle that horse and get yourself up here."

He could not think of anything more to say, so he did like she said. He removed the bridle and turned the horse loose to graze and water. He was still scared to death of the girl, and his legs began to tremble as he mounted the porch steps. She followed with her eyes, wondering for a moment if he would trip and fall. Nate made it onto the porch and saw that she looked even prettier up close.

She tipped back in the chair again to study him, raising a leg to rest her foot on the chair.

"What's your name, Deputy?"

"Nathan Osterhaus, ma'am."

"Louisa Charles Foster. You can sit if you want."

Nate stared at her raised leg and realized if she had drawn it a little higher he would be able to see if she was wearing underwear. Such an idea had never occurred to him before, but he was overwhelmed by a sudden rush of desire to know whether she was, and if so what in the world it might look like. He boldly stepped toward a chair on the opposite side of the beer tub where he could see for himself. She lowered the leg as he sat, and leaned over to pull a beer from the tub. She removed the wire from the cork and tossed the bottle to him.

He looked unsure of what to do with it.

"Here, let me open that," she said.

He held the bottle to her in both hands, and she pulled it with the corkscrew. He took a swallow and nodded appreciation. She leaned back in her chair and took a pull on her own beer, but did not raise her leg again.

Nate was hers now, unable to take his eyes off her.

"Where are you from, Nathan Osterhaus?"

"Cleburne. We're on a manhunt for a fellow killed his wife."

"Do you have a girlfriend?"

He was too scared of her to lie. "No. I've never had one."

She was not shocked. "Too bad. There's a lot about you for some lucky girl to like."

"My mother says I'm too young for girls. She won't let me anywhere near them except sometimes at church. I've talked to a few when there's grown-ups around but that's about it."

"Have you ever kissed one?"

"No, but I touched one once. She slapped me so silly I couldn't see for about a minute." Louisa looked at him and saw he was serious.

"Now, that's sad," she said, with another sip of her beer. "I think girls like that are tragic. They live unhappy lives and ruin a lot of boys for other girls."

"Do you have a boyfriend?" He could not imagine that she did not have fifteen or twenty.

"Out here? What do you think? Well, I have boyfriends that Daddy doesn't know about sometimes, but they never stay long. Nobody comes here unless they're on the way to someplace else. Not that I blame them. After my mother died, Daddy didn't want to farm cotton anymore so he sold the place and decided to do this."

"Is it a living?"

"Well, it's a shortcut to Bottle's Pass. We can only operate about six months of the year, but that's usually enough. The river's too high in the spring and we move back to town in winter, so we just have summer. Sometimes you won't see anybody for a month. Other times it's like the whole world wants across at once. That's when we make our money."

"It's nice enough out here."

"Wake up, Nathan. It's boring, boring, boring! Daddy doesn't know it yet but I won't be here much longer. I deserve a life while I'm still young. I intend to find one out there somewhere."

"How do you figure on doing that?"

"Steal his money and leave. Daddy will be upset but he'll get over it."

"Where do you intend to go?"

She shrugged. "I talk to people. They come from all over, on the way to everywhere. Some say I can look them up if I ever get out their way. Probably I'll find out if they mean it or not. Anyway I learn things from them.

Once I decide what I want, I'll be gone. It won't be long now."

"I've been thinking along those lines myself," Nate said, reaching for a second beer and twisting off the wire. He held it out for her to pull the cork, and then drank. The alcohol took the edge off his nerves. "You have the jump on me because you learn stuff out here. I intend to pick up things on these manhunts. Truth is, I'm seventeen and don't hardly know anything. Mama's interested in religion and stuff, but that's got nothing to do with this world."

They talked late into the afternoon, and Louisa fixed them a light dinner to eat on the porch in the peaceful riverside twilight.

"It's too dangerous to try to fetch the ferry now," she said. "You can stay in my room. Daddy's bed is smelly but I'm used to it. We'll get the ferry at daybreak and have you on your way."

That night Nate lay awake in the darkness of Louisa's bedroom. He had never slept in a girl's bed before. It was softer than any he had known and smelled nice. With the gentle whisper of the river outside, he ought to have conked right out, but Nate could not get Louisa out of his head. It had been exciting to talk with her all afternoon. He had always wondered what girls were like and what kinds of stuff they thought about and how they felt about things. He lay in her bed and rolled these things around in his head until he drifted off.

Nate was asleep less than an hour when something woke him. He lay very still and listened intensely. It was less than a noise, more like a presence. Abruptly her hot breath was in his ear, and he felt her soft nakedness over his body as she slid into bed. His body caught fire against hers. He did not understand what was happening. It mattered not, because she was confident and sure, and showed him what to do, and for the remainder of the night they could not get enough of each other.

Nate awoke at daybreak to the feel of a naked girl against his body, asleep and breathing quietly. He lay experiencing the moment and did not want it to ever end.

Eventually she began to stir, and shortly after that rolled over on top of him. She pushed her hair back from her face so she could kiss him sweetly.

"Morning, Deputy."

Their faces were almost touching. "Damn, Louisa," he said. "I was always interested in girls but never knew they could do—well—all that stuff."

She ran a hand through his hair. "It's too bad you have to leave. Daddy won't be back for a few more days."

Nate pushed her off and she squealed as he rolled over on top of her. He looked down into her shining face.

"Who said I was in a hurry? Hell, it's not like the world's going to end tomorrow!"

The posse had spent two days negotiating the rock-strewn slopes of Dug's Gap, and the men were starting to lose enthusiasm. Bob, encouraged by a discarded whiskey bottle and a tin can recently emptied of beans, was confident Jessup had passed this way. He felt sure Sheriff Briscoe's posse had already captured the bastard a little further ahead.

When they emerged from the gap, nothing lay before them but desert and scrub. Bob now figured Arlan must have taken Jessup back to Fedora, and turned south to follow. He came upon Briscoe's posse the next day; six men deployed across the egress of Bottle's Pass, where they had lain under a scorching sun for several days. Bob studied them for a minute and then shook his head. He dismounted and walked over to discuss the blunder with Arlan. The men of both posses had begun to get surly after days of pursuit in the hot sun with no trace of a fugitive. Bob and Arlan decided to camp there for the night and figure something out in the morning.

Shortly after sunrise, a rider out of Fedora arrived with the telegram from McCook instructing Briscoe to move to Dug's Gap. It was now that Arlan's boys learned of the mix-up. One of them called Bob's posse the dumbest sons of bitches he ever saw. Jeff Haskell, who had been fed up for several days now, punched the fellow in the mouth. The two men went to ground, with Jeff on top pummeling the other one in the face. The fellow underneath drew his pistol and stuck Jeff across the side of the head to knock him off. Then he rolled on top of Jeff and started to pistol-whip him.

It took several boys from both posses to pull them apart. Arlan's man had lost a tooth, and Jeff was bleeding from a gash across the side of his head. They were caked with blood and dirt. Captain Schoepff advised the sheriffs that their men were too out of sorts to be worth much in a further pursuit. Bob and Arlan agreed it was best under the circumstances to write this whole thing off. Briscoe's bunch departed south to Fedora, and Bob took his men east into Bottle's Pass.

Bob's posse returned to Cleburne two weeks after having embarked on a manhunt into high desert. They had not fired a shot and were one man short. Folks watching them pass in the street remarked about how tired and caked with dust everybody looked. The horses were pretty fagged out too.

"Did you catch him?" somebody shouted from the sidewalk.

"Go to hell!" Blewitt said.

The posse disbanded quietly, each man going his own way without so much as a word to the others.

Dorothea was grateful to see her husband walk through the door alive and in one piece, but knew at a glance not to ask how things had gone. Bob emptied his rifle and put it back in the gun rack, and asked if she would fix him some eggs for breakfast. He said that he was going to shave and bathe, and after a hot breakfast intended to catch up on his sleep for a few days.

"Still nothing about Eddie Lee on the wire," she said, as she started for the kitchen.

"I never want to hear that name again for as long as I live," Bob said. "The hell with the bastard. As far as I'm concerned I've never met him, do not know him, and never even heard of the man."

Bob was in the bathhouse, where he had taken off his shirt and was shaving at a mirror, when Dorothea looked in the door.

"Alice Osterhaus is here and wants to see you," she said.

"Oh, hell. I need to get some rest. Tell her to come back tomorrow."

"No, you'd better talk to her now. She's about to have an attack of the fits over Nate."

Bob sighed. He walked back to the house without setting down the razor or putting on a shirt. His grizzled face was only half-shaven.

Alice was too distraught to notice his appearance. "Bob, I want to know what you've done with my boy. Why isn't he back with the others?"

"I don't know where he is, Alice."

"You need to tell me what happened out there! Was there a shoot-out?"

"No, we didn't have a damn shoot-out."

"Then where is he?"

Bob sighed. "I sent him to deliver a telegram to McCook. That was a week ago, and it was the last I saw of him. I told him to go home after that."

"Well, he sure hasn't shown up."

"Alice, it took that boy four days to make a ten-hour ride to McCook. Go figure for yourself how long he'll need to find Cleburne."

The sheriff looked pretty upset about whatever had happened on the prairie, but she was skeptical about his story. "There's something very fishy about all this, Bob," she said. "I'm going to go ask the telegraph office if you're telling me the truth. They'll know if he was really in McCook."

"Oh, he was there, all right."

"You can expect big trouble if he wasn't. I know my Nate. He always comes straight home."

She slammed the door and was gone. Bob stood half shaven with no shirt and still holding the razor. He was dirty and tired and fed up. He opened the door and called to her.

"If he shows up, you'd best let me know," he said. "I need to lock him in a cell a few days until my posse cools down. Otherwise you might see a shoot-out right here in Cleburne!"

WHY MEN CHEAT IN AUGUST

It was the first week of August, and Ed Hawn's wife came upon a curious letter in the morning mail. The plain white envelope looked harmless enough, mixed in with a couple of magazines and some junk mail, until she noticed it was hand addressed to her husband in penciled block letters. There was no return address on either side. She sniffed at it, but it had no scent.

Patsy had a bad feeling about this. She and Ed had been married twenty-seven years, and in all that time nothing like this had ever come to the house. The envelope was not even of stationery quality. It looked like those cheap ones sold in the school supply aisle of drugstores that inflict a paper cut when licked. She spotted a pink smudge along the edge of the flap, but was not sure it was blood. The sender might have deposited a speck of lipstick while licking the envelope, and then wiped it off with a finger.

No, Patsy decided, she did not like this one bit. She went into the house and put the letter on the desk with the rest of the mail. She was not going to say anything to Ed about it. He got home from the law office a little after six and always looked through the mail first thing. She wanted to see if he was going to bring it up.

Patsy was fixing a dinner salad in the kitchen when the front door slammed shortly after six. She listened for the sound of her husband shuffling through the mail like he always did. But Ed walked past the desk as if it were not there, and went straight to the kitchen to find his wife.

"Bobby Dosher is selling his horse," he said, without so much as a hello.

"Who's Bobby Dosher?"

"You've met him. He owns that bay mare, Bambam. I've had my eye on her for a while now."

"Oh, for God's sake. Ed, you're not going to buy another horse."

"Now that I'm president of the cutting association, I need to start doing better in the arena. I could run up some points on this lady."

"I swear to God, I'm starting to feel sorry you ever got mixed up with those people."

Patsy and Ed had lived together happily for many years, and raised two grown boys, without either of them being aware cutting horses even existed. She had looked forward to the day when the kids were out of school, Ed was retired, and they could travel the world together. She dreamed of exploring the Greek island of Santorini, and sunning lazily on the beaches of the French Riviera, and then moving on to endless other adventures.

One day a client named Norbert Anderson who owed Ed a lot of money asked if he'd accept a champion cutting horse named Duchess in payment of the debt. Patsy did not think her husband ought to accept a horse in return for legal services. But Norbert was a good talker, and the next thing she knew, Ed was in the thrall of the sport of cutting cows from a herd on horseback.

Truthfully, he showed little natural ability for the pursuit, but this relic of the Old West so excited him that she soon grew weary of listening to him talk about it. She also thought it embarrassing, almost inappropriate, for a man his age to ride in Amateur class, where he mostly competed against teenaged girls from the local high school. Patsy was not jealous because she knew Ed was intimidated by girls that age, and had not been able to get a date with one even in high school. The young riders Roy Halibut recruited to jump-start Ginger Witt's new cutting association were nice enough, and even gave him riding tips, but Ed was anxious to shed them by moving into Non-Pro. He had purchased several horses in search of the one that would make him a weekend champion, and two of them still boarded in a makeshift paddock and weather shelter in the backyard.

"I see where this is headed," Patsy said over dinner that evening. "You have no intention of traveling the world with me after retirement. You want to sell this house and move us into the country someplace where you can stable cutting horses."

Patsy's mother had advised her to indulge her husband in his new interest, because he was at the age when some married men begin hanging in bars where young girls come looking for trouble. But Patsy knew she need not share those concerns of other women. Ed had learned early in life that women did not find him interesting. Patsy was pretty sure he had not been on a date until the day he hired her as secretary at his first law office. She was confident Ed did not know anything about women she had not taught him. Patsy had spotted him as a cheat-proof man in a secure profession. He was a good provider and family man who always came home at night. While she wasn't worried he might run off with a teenaged cutter, she did feel a man his age ought to spend more time at home with his wife.

"Patsy, let's not fuss about this," Ed said. He finished his plate and pushed back from the table, wiping his face with a napkin. "I need to run out to see Bobby Dosher. It won't take long."

"You're going to leave me here by myself tonight to go look at a horse?"

"I've been thinking about it all day. I want to be sure about this."

"You haven't even checked the mail yet." She had almost forgotten the letter, but seized upon it now.

"I can do that later."

"No, I think you should look at it now," she said suddenly.

Ed sensed something not right. "Is there something I should see?"

"You tell me. I don't know your business."

He went into the living room to the desk. She followed and watched as he flipped through the mail. He paused at the plain white envelope with penciled block letters.

"What's this?"

"It's not addressed to me."

Ed had no idea what it might be, but an uneasy feeling came over him that maybe he ought not to open it in front of his wife.

"What's wrong, Ed? Is it something you don't want me to see?"

Confident it could not possibly be anything he needed to keep from his wife, he opened it. Ed frowned and read it several times to make sure he was not misunderstanding something.

"Well? What does it say?"

He shook his head. "I'm not sure, exactly. It's cutting horse association business."

"Why did it come to the house?"

"I guess because I'm president." He started to put it back in the envelope, when Patsy snatched it from his hand.

It was written in the same penciled block letters as the address:

THAT BITCH KIT IS SLEEPING WITH DYLAN PARKER. SHE NEEDS TO BE KICKED OUT OF AMATEUR.

"Who's Kit?" she said.

Ed quickly took it back and pushed it into the envelope. "This is confidential. You weren't supposed to see that."

"I have a right to know what's going on in my own house."

"Somebody is complaining about one of our members."

"I don't doubt that for a minute."

"It's a challenge to the eligibility of a contestant."

"It's kind of trashy."

"Patsy, this is a technical issue," he said. "I'll pass it along to the board, and they'll handle it."

Patsy was not satisfied. "How well do you know this Kit? And who's Dylan Parker?"

"She rides Amateur and he's her trainer." He sighed.

"It sounds trashy to me. A man your age needs to be careful about his reputation. I don't like you getting mixed up with —"

"I'm not mixed up with anything," Ed said. "I told you, it's a matter for the board. I'll submit it to them and that'll be the end of it."

Patsy suspected there was more to this than he was letting on. Ed refused to discuss it further. However, he decided not to go to Bobby Dosher's place to see

Bambam that night. He needed to stay home and make some phone calls.

— ii —

Ed called an emergency meeting of the board of the Inland Empire Cutting Horse Association on a Sunday afternoon in his law offices above the Wells Fargo Bank in downtown Ramone. Only six of nine officers of the fledgling association were able to appear on such short notice, but seated around the table in his conference room they constituted a quorum.

"This better be important," Phil McKnealey said. "My wife's relatives are visiting from Oklahoma, and she's not very happy with me. We were supposed to take them to see Anaheim today." Phil owned the Allstate Insurance franchise in an office down the hall and had known Ed for years. He was the show/events secretary in charge of scheduling and securing locations for their cuttings.

"It's pitiful to drag people away from family on a weekend like this," Ed said. "But something has come up that I feel needs the immediate attention of the board."

Normally the board convened on the second Friday of each month at a local bar or restaurant to discuss association business over drinks. Nothing like this had happened before, and everyone waited for Ed to explain himself. He opened his briefcase and removed a ringbound notebook of national cutting horse association regulations which he set to one side. Then he took out the anonymous envelope.

"This came to my house in the mail," he said, removing the letter. "Personally I'm not convinced there's a whole lot to this. But it raises an important issue, and I feel it is my duty as president to submit it to you for review."

Phil sat on his left and reached for the letter, but Ed gave it to Vice President and Treasurer Ginger Witt to his right. Ginger was a red-haired, sun-weathered divorcee in her mid-forties who bred quarter horses on a ranch near Yucaipa. She was the financial engine that drove the fledgling organization, and for that reason the most important person in the room.

Ginger's divorce from a Hollywood actor some years back made tabloid headlines and alienated her from her children, but left her with the financial wherewithal to pursue a passion for horses. She claimed to have sworn off men and had no personal life so far as anyone knew. The hard knocks of life had thickened her skin, and a generous judgment by a divorce court permitted her the indulgence of having her way, for which she was notorious. It was said of Ginger that she might have a falling out with a billionaire over horses as casually as other people complained about cold coffee to a waitress. The ranch she had owned in the Santa Ynez had been mired in litigation arising from disputes with neighbors, prominent individuals in the horse industry, and a local cutting association. She became so disgusted with horse people in the central portion of the state that she told a judge there she wouldn't piss on the Paso Robles Event Center if it caught on fire.

Not long after that she sold her Santa Ynez property and purchased a ranch in San Bernardino County. While there was less of a market for cutting horses here, she intended to build up one that was under her total control. She encouraged local interest in cutting and founded the Inland Empire Cutting Horse Association, or IECHA/CutAway, together with Ed Hawn and others from local cuttings she sponsored. An all-weather enclosed arena was under construction on her ranch to host association events, and she was committed to funding the association until operations generated enough revenue to be self-supporting. Her purpose was to create a venue for showing horses bred or trained on her ranch, and to develop a local interest and market for the sport to rival any other in the state. Though she had only one vote, how she felt on a matter carried undue weight with the board.

Ginger calmly retrieved a pair of reading glasses from her purse and studied the anonymous letter. Everyone looked for some sense of her opinion, but of this her expressionless face gave no hint. She quietly folded the letter and passed it without comment to Stuart Larkin on her right.

Stu was a young high school teacher and cutting enthusiast along with his wife Sandy. He wrote the association newsletter, approved vendors at events, and solicited sponsors from the local business community. With no hint from Ginger for guidance, he absorbed the letter in thoughtful silence and then passed it to Roy Halibut.

Roy's reaction was startled disbelief. He looked again to make sure he saw right, and then sat back and began to chuckle, and shook his head.

"I see somebody is enjoying this," Ginger said.

"No, no! I'm sorry, Ginger. Say, it's - this is serious business," he said, struggling to contain himself. "It's a good thing Ed called us up here on a Sunday afternoon to see this."

Roy was easily the most experienced, but least wealthy, horseman in the room. Though notoriously popular with the ladies, the hard life and low wages of a ranch hand had kept him single. He was well-liked and on a first-name basis with a lot of local farmers and ranchers, and these connections made him essential to the association as their one-man cattle committee. Roy assured they always had the necessary number of cows to work at events.

He was still shaking his head when he passed the letter to Jack Pardee. Jack owned the local Toyota dealership and was in the middle of a weekend blowout sale to clear his lot for next year's models. Like Phil, he was not happy about being here.

Jack considered the letter. "This is about Kitty Trotka?"

"That would appear to be the case," Ed said uneasily.

Kitty was a local girl recently graduated from high school who worked in town and competed in Amateur class. She was well positioned to win the Amateur cutting championship at the end of IECHA's first operating year.

"Let me see that thing," Phil McKnealey said. Jack handed it to him, and Phil scrutinized it for something the others might have missed. He looked up and frowned at Ed. "You called us here on a weekend for this?"

"Finals are coming up pretty quick now," Ed said. "It would look bad if IECHA's first Amateur champion turned out to be ineligible. If we're going to disqualify somebody, we need to do it now."

"Look, I'm pretty sure I know what's going on here," Roy said. "Phil, let me have that letter. Everybody else can go on home. I'll take care of this."

Phil started to pass the letter across the table, but Ginger snatched it. "Don't give that to him!" she said. "Roy, you're acting like this is some kind of joke. If you know something about this, you need to share it with the board."

"It's pretty obvious what's going on," Roy said. "Kitty's got a lock on Amateur. She's so far out on points nobody's going to catch her unless she's disqualified."

"Are you suggesting a spiteful competitor sent this?" Ed said.

"I know damn well who sent it. It doesn't take a genius. Gretchen Tankersley is in second, and that headstrong little scamp would trip her own grandmother down a flight of stairs to take Amateur."

"Can you prove that?" Ginger said.

"Give me the letter. Let me show it to Gretchen. I know that girl very, very well. She'll own up to it if I confront her."

"I say we go along with Fish on this one," Phil said. "Let him run with it, and let's get out of here."

"I'm not sure we can do that, Phil," Ed said. He was studying the regulations in the ringed binder. "There's nothing in here authorizing us to seek the identity of the complaining party."

"What does it say?" Jack said.

"Anyone believing a member is in violation of regulations may complain by anonymous letter to the president. The board may dismiss the allegations if it deems them not credible, or it may appoint a committee of at least two members to investigate further." Ed looked up. "I'm sorry, Roy."

Roy slumped back in his chair and shook his head.

"Point of information," Phil said. "Can somebody be kicked out of Amateur for sleeping with her trainer?"

"That's a good question," Ed said. "I'm still new at this, but if we want our events to count toward state and national titles, we have to follow their regulations." He leafed through the notebook.

"Don't try to lawyer up on us, Ed," Ginger said. "Dylan Parker is a married man, even if he is separated from his wife. If this girl is involved with him it makes us look bad."

Ed put his finger on a page. "Here's the rule. A contestant may not ride Amateur class if said person lives and works on a professional cutting horse ranch, or if said person cohabits with a professional."

"Kitty lives in town," Stu said. "She sublets a room near that restaurant where she works."

"If she's sleeping with Parker, that's cohabiting," Ginger said.

"Ginger, I believe a person's mailing address is generally accepted as their place of residence," Ed said.

"I get my mail at the post office," she said. "Are you telling me I live in a PO box?"

"What's the definition of cohabit?" Jack asked.

"I have a dictionary on the bookshelf." Ed started to get it.

Phil consulted his smartphone. "Cohabit. To coexist. Animals that coexist with humans thrive."

Ginger was on her own phone as well. "Cohabit. To have a sexual relationship without being married."

"That sounds like a colloquial definition," Ed said.

"I think the rule is ambiguous," Jack said.

Stuart began to say something, but Roy sank his head into his arms on the table and began to shake with helpless laughter.

Ginger glared at him. Roy could not stop laughing.

"Roy, I wish you wouldn't even show up at these meetings if you don't have something to contribute," she said.

"We need to move on here," Ed added, uneasily.

Roy pulled himself together enough to sit up. "I'm sorry, everybody," he said. "Go ahead, Stuart."

"I taught Kitty in high school and had a high opinion of her," Stuart said. "What's more, I'm not very comfortable about this. We're a cutting association. We have no authority to investigate people's personal lives."

"Stuart's point is well-taken," Ed said. "We ought to resolve this with a simple vote. Personally I find the letter thin on specifics. I suggest we dismiss it, and let's everybody forget the whole thing and go home."

"I've got something to say about that," Ginger said. "I'm investing a lot of money in this operation, and I don't like what I'm hearing one bit. We all know Kitty Trotka will be our first Amateur champion come November. What happens if it turns out she wasn't eligible? We'll be the laughingstock of the state. We don't need that kind of scandal."

"Ginger, we haven't got anything but a piece of paper," Phil said.

Ginger began flipping through photos of events on her smartphone. She found one of Kitty and Dylan Parker at a cutting. She held up the phone for everyone to see and then passed it around the table. "Phil, I want you to look at this. Don't tell me there's nothing going on between them."

Phil studied it doubtfully. "They're just sitting together," he said. "It doesn't look like they're even talking."

"Those sassy tits do the talking," Ginger said. "Anyway, it's August. This kind of stuff always gets started in August."

"What's August got to do with it?" Ed said.

"My father left us in August," Ginger said. "My mother always told me that's when you need to keep an eye on a man. I wish I'd followed that advice. I caught two ex-husbands between the sheets with those little skanks in August."

There was a moment of silence around the table.

"My wife got me in January," Jack Pardee said.

Ed sighed. He wanted to wrap this thing up. "Well, so far all we've got is an anonymous letter and the fact it's August."

"I need to get home," Phil said. "Can we put this to a vote?"

"All right. How many feel the allegations merit further study?" Ed said.

Ginger promptly shot up her hand. She gave Ed a hard look. "We can't dismiss an accusation like this without an investigation. Ed, I'm going to be very disappointed if you don't show some leadership and protect the reputation of the association."

Reluctantly, Ed raised his hand, and it was two of six.

Ginger was an important client of Phil's equine insurance business, so he raised his hand as well.

Stu shook his head. "Ginger, I have to abstain." She gave him a stern look but said nothing.

Jack, wary of Ginger's displeasure, also raised his hand.

Roy was tipped back in his chair, following the vote with a bemused look, but said nothing.

"For the record, do we have any opposed?" Ed said.

Only Roy raised his hand.

"The motion passes with four yeses, one no, and one abstention," Ed said. "Now we just need to appoint a committee and we can get out of here. Volunteers?"

Ginger shot up her hand. There was no one else.

"Stu, since you abstained, you would make a good impartial investigator."

"Sorry, Ed. I want no part of this."

"We need a committee of at least two," Ed said. "Jack, how about you?"

"I'm not going to ask Dylan Parker if he's doing Kitty. He's sore enough about his wife divorcing him. I might get my teeth knocked out."

"We should leave Parker out of this," Ginger said. "The complaint is against Kitty."

"I have another point of information," Phil said. "I don't even know what an investigative committee is supposed to do, exactly."

Roy sat up and showed interest again. "I have some ideas," he said.

"Roy, you didn't even vote for it," Ginger said.

"No, we're open to suggestions here," Ed said. "Go ahead, Fish."

"I think the committee ought to go out to Parker's house while he's at work. Look through the trash cans to see how many whiskey bottles and beer cans he's got in there. Knock on a few doors and ask neighbors if there's been loud music and partying carrying on to all hours of the night."

"I sure wish you'd go home," Ginger said.

Her aggravation only encouraged him. "You might also talk to Kitty's landlady. Ask if she's been dragging in like the cat at all hours, or if the postman's complained about mail accumulating in her box."

"Roy, you're giving me a headache," Ginger said. "We need one more person to fill out the committee."

Phil reminded her that his wife's relatives were in town, and Jack was in the middle of a blowout sale. Stuart had already made clear he wanted no part of it. Roy said that since the board had passed on all his suggestions, he would leave the investigation to experts.

Ginger looked frustrated. "All right," she said. "I nominate Ed Hawn."

Ed looked startled. "Ginger, this is a volunteer position. You can't nominate somebody."

"I just did. If somebody will second it, we can adjourn."

"Seconded!" Roy said, raising his hand with a grin.

"Fish, don't do that!" Ed said.

"Hey, it's your letter," Roy said. "Anyway you voted to investigate this thing."

"Are we done here?" Phil asked.

"Fine," Ed said with a sigh. "We're adjourned."

"Well, hallelujah!" Roy said. He got up and drifted to the door. Phil and Jack pushed past him and were gone.

Ed started putting things in his carrying case to leave.

"Ed, don't even think about going anywhere," Ginger said.

"I was hoping to spend what's left of the afternoon with my wife."

"Patsy can wait. We're on committee now, and we're not going anywhere until we figure out how to proceed with this." Ginger leaned back, swung her dusty boots onto the table, and felt for the pack of cigarettes in her shirt pocket.

Roy paused to wink at Ed from the door. "Ed, we're all depending on you and Ginger to get to the bottom of this thing, you hear?" Roy closed the door quietly and they were alone.

"Ginger, I really do need to get home," Ed said. "Patsy says I'm more interested in horses than my own wife. If she finds out I'm investigating teenaged girls, I'm in real trouble."

"Do you have a bottle in here or do we have to hit a bar?"

— iii —

Ginger did not feel sorry for anybody. Ed sighed and went to the bookshelf. He got down on hands and knees to open a cabinet door, pulled out the stack of ledgers that concealed his liquor, and peered into the dark opening. "We have whiskey, vodka, and a little scotch."

"Scotch," she said, lighting up a cigarette. "I'll bet there's a damn ashtray in there, too."

Ed brought over the scotch, two glasses, and an ash tray. He poured them each half a glass and set the bottle on the table. She sniffed at the glass, and tried it.

"This isn't half-bad, Ed."

"Gift from a client. Patsy won't let me keep liquor in the office so I had to hide it. Now I've got a whole little hooch collection down there. I don't believe a man ought to keep things from his wife, but it's only a little secret."

"What do you want to do about Kitty?" Ginger said.

Ed fingered his scotch miserably. "Ginger, let me tell you the honest truth," he said. "I wish to God the minute I saw that letter, I'd just crumpled it up and thrown it into the trash. That would have been the end of it. But it came while I was at work and then Patsy saw it. Horses don't interest her, so she doesn't believe teenaged girls go to cuttings for the horses. That's why it looked so bad when this letter came to the house. I told her it was horse association business and I'd have the board take care of it. Now look where that's got me. Good God, I'm on the investigative committee!"

Ginger exhaled smoke and looked up at the ceiling. "How well do you know Kitty?"

"Hardly at all, actually. She's a waitress at the Cactus Rose Café, and rents a room in town with some other girl. Her parents bought that horse for her and she rides in most every cutting. People seem to like her. She's a fine young lady to my knowledge."

"I know all about girls that age and don't like her one bit. If we don't disqualify her, she's going to take Amateur."

"Dylan Parker is a thirty-five-year-old man and married to boot, even if he is separated from his wife. I find it hard to believe a nineteen-year-old girl would get involved with someone like that."

"She'd drop her drawers for him in a heartbeat," Ginger said.

"That's harsh. Anyway, what if she did? It would be a fling. That's not cohabitation."

"Ed, I can't remember the last time I saw a grown man so ignorant about women. You think just because they're teenagers, these girls are angels. I'm here to tell you they're not. Once a woman turns thirty-five, she has to really look out for those little pests. Don't tell me I don't know what I'm talking about."

Ed looked miserable. "I believe Roy is right," he said. "What we've got here is a vindictive schoolgirl who wants first place when she's only got second. I wish to God we'd let Roy confront Gretchen Tankersly like he wanted."

"I'm the one paying the bills," Ginger said. "The awards barbecue will be here before you know it, and *Quarter Horse News* is sending somebody to cover it. This is a very big deal for us."

They sat in silence a moment. Ed changed the subject. "How's the covered arena coming along?"

"Over budget and behind schedule like everything else in this world."

The investigative committee was at an impasse.

They finished the scotch around sundown, and Ed got the vodka from his hooch cabinet. There were several cigarette butts in Ginger's ashtray. She sat with her boots on the table and blew cigarette smoke into the air.

"Here's an aggravating story for you," she said. "I saw in the tabloids where Scott Ballard bought a villa on Lake Como. He's vacationing out there with his third wife. That ought to be me. We were a couple of kids when I married him. He was damn good-looking for an unemployed young actor nobody'd ever heard of. We had to mix corn flakes with the hamburger to get by, but we did some crazy things and had a lot of fun, I have to admit. It took seven years for the right part to come along, and overnight we were Hollywood royalty. That's when all the barely legal little floozies - you think they're goddamn angels, but they're not – came out of the woodwork. I knew he was doing them, what man wouldn't? Al Goldman, that was his agent at the time, told me to hang in there because it was just a phase. If I'd followed that advice I'd be sunning on the shores of Lake Como with Scott Ballard today. Do you know the son of a bitch is the second highest-paid actor in the world? Well, I guarantee you this much. I've owned some good horses and some bad horses, but not a goddamned one ever cheated on me."

Ed rarely had more than one drink, if that, on a Sunday, but he finished his vodka like it was a glass of water. His head sank miserably into his arms on the table. "Ginger, I'm sorry about this, but I just don't have any more ideas. I wish I could wake up with a big hangover tomorrow and have somebody shake me to say this thing has gone away."

Ginger poured a little more vodka in their glasses.

"I have a proposition for you," she said. "If you want out of this, let's put her to a little test. Stay with me on this, Ed. Let's declare the awards barbecue a celebration of Amateurs because they're our future. The Amateur champion will be princess of the event. I'll open my checkbook and buy some high-end couture that'll make her sparkle and shine. She might even land on the cover of *Quarter Horse News*."

"I like that idea a lot," Ed said. For a fleeting moment he was relieved by this new drift of thought.

"Kitty has a lock on Amateur so she's the one we're talking about. Seems to me as president, you should run this past her to make sure she's up to it."

"I'll call her tomorrow."

"No, I want you to go down to the Cactus Rose Café and ask her to have dinner with you, so the two of you can work out the details in person."

"Dinner?" Ed frowned.

"Buena Hacienda Inn ought to impress her."

"Ginger, I can't ask a nineteen-year-old girl for a dinner date. I'm a middle-aged married man. It wouldn't be appropriate. Anyway, she wouldn't do it."

"She'll do it in a heartbeat. I know all about these girls. She won't turn down the president of CutAway."

"I'll have to give this some thought."

"When you make the reservations, I want you to book a room for the night. Tell the concierge to put a bottle of this scotch and two glasses on the nightstand."

"A room for what?" Ed gave her a startled look.

"I'll buy some nice things for our Amateur champion to wear and have them sent to your office. Put them on the bed in the hotel room. Then over dinner, tell her that I said for her to try them on for size."

"Ginger, she's not going to go up to a hotel room with a married man."

"She'll go. The minute that skinny little strumpet sees that bottle of scotch on the nightstand, she'll put two and two together and figure out what's going on. That little trollop's going to be all over you."

"I can't believe we're even discussing this! I wouldn't have any idea how to handle a situation like that."

She laughed. "Ed, I'm pretty sure you can peel loose

from a teenaged tart. Then go to the front desk and have her thrown out for misbehaving. We'll have the board expel her from CutAway for propositioning the president."

Ed struggled with the feeling he was hopelessly out of his depth. "I believe this is misguided. Stuart taught her in high school and says...."

"If Stu's right, and she blows you off, I will personally recommend the board drop the investigation. That's what you want, isn't it? Well, there's my proposal."

He was appalled but wanted in the worst way to bring this thing to an end.

"I'll have to ask Patsy about this."

"Patsy doesn't need to know about it. You lied to her about the goddamn scotch, didn't you? Tell her you need to see a man about a horse that night."

Ed was getting scared now, but he was too tired to argue anymore. He did not understand how a simple letter in the mail could have gone so haywire on him.

Ed showed up at home after dark on a Sunday evening with alcohol on his breath and told Patsy the anonymous letter had gone to committee for study. When she asked why it had taken so long, he said everybody got to talking about horses and lost track of time.

— iv —

Ed left his office early Monday afternoon, and sat in a bar across the street from the Cactus Rose Café. He was waiting for the lunch crowd to die down so he could approach Kitty. He believed Ginger was off the rails about this, and Kitty would never agree to a dinner date with him. The few girls he had found the courage to ask out in his youth had looked startled or even offended by the suggestion. Nonetheless, he had to go through with this. It was the only way Ginger would agree to dismiss the confounded letter.

He intended to order something non-alcoholic while waiting, but the prospect of asking Kitty for a date proved more intimidating than expected. Girls had blown off poor Ed too many times in younger days. The thought of subjecting himself to yet another such humiliation after so many years was unsettling. He fortified his courage with a whiskey.

Ed's mind raced with frightening ways Kitty might react. He imagined her mouth falling open as she stared at him in wide-eyed disbelief. What if she laughed in his face? Suppose, God forbid, she turned and shouted to everyone in the café that Ed Hawn had just asked her for a date? The room would explode with laughter as he slinked out the door, and after that people would be telling jokes about him all over town. But Ed felt he had no choice if he wanted to end the investigation.

The Cactus Rose lunch rush was over at two o'clock. From the bar, Ed could see Kitty and two other waitresses cleaning tables across the street. He had numbed his nerves with alcohol, and pushed away a half-finished second glass because he did not want to appear intoxicated. Ed slid from the barstool and was grateful to discover he felt steady on his feet. Next, he casually exited the bar, and while crossing the street, felt confident he looked normal to anyone who might be watching. This was going to be all right, he told himself.

Kitty was wiping the counter when Ed entered the café; a cocktail mix of dread, anxiety and alcohol shot through his body like a lightning bolt and numbed him to a frazzle. He flushed hot all over, and wanted to run out the door in blind panic, but was unable to move.

"Oh, hi Ed!" Kitty said brightly, as she looked up from her work. "Grab a seat. I'll get a menu. You want coffee?"

He stood paralyzed in the doorway and stared at her with an awkward lopsided grin. Kitty was an athletic dark-haired girl with sun-bronzed skin and a wholesome personality. Anybody would want a date with her.

"Hey, guys!" she said. "Look who came to see us. This is Ed Hawn. He's president of CutAway."

The other two girls knew about Kitty's riding interests and responded with warm smiles and waves. Good God, I'm drunk as a skunk and they don't know it, Ed thought. But the friendly welcome and acknowledgment of his importance in Kitty's cutting club lifted his confidence. The rush of panic and intoxication subsided as abruptly it had arisen. Kitty approached with a menu and coffeepot.

"No, it's fine, Kitty," he said, attempting an air of assured dignity. "I was just passing by and thought you might like to hear a little CutAway news."

"Oh, sure! What's up?"

"The board is working on the awards barbecue and has come up with some exciting ideas. We believe Amateurs are the future of the sport and decided to theme the event around them."

"Really?" Kitty's eyes sparkled. "Amateur? Wow, that's me!"

"How do you like it?"

"I'm not sure what the Non-Pros will say. But, yeah, it's super cool with me," she said with a laugh.

"Well, the way you've been riding, everybody is looking at you for Amateur. I should probably fill you in on this. Why don't you have dinner with me tonight at Buena Hacienda?"

"Tonight?"

"Does seven o'clock work for you?"

Kitty gave him an all-too-familiar look of pained disappointment. "Aww, I can't," she said. "I don't get off until eleven. I'm sorry."

Ed was on a roller-coaster ride which had crested for a brief moment, only to have his world crumble as it plunged into a steep descent.

"Oh, sure!" he said quickly. "No, I understand." The coaster leveled off with a rush of relief that she had let him off easy. He was grateful to her for being so decent about this and not humiliating him. His job was done here; the investigation was complete and his dignity intact. He turned to leave.

"What about tomorrow?" Kitty said.

Ed froze in the doorway. His ears turned bright red and rang loudly as he struggled to make sure he heard right. She did not correct herself.

"Tomorrow would be fine," he said. The words stumbled out awkwardly as he grappled with the unexpected turn of events.

"I'm off around six or six-thirty, depending on how busy we are."

"It looks like dinner reservations for seven then," he said.

"Thanks, Ed. This is exciting. I'll see you there!"

Ed's mind was swimming as he left the café. It was the first time in his life a girl had said yes to a date with him. His heart almost began to soar, but he quickly grappled it to earth, reminding himself who he was and that it wasn't actually a date. Still it felt like one, and he allowed himself to pretend it was, and saw no harm in that. He believed every man ought to experience the feeling when a pretty girl says yes to a date at least once in his life. For Ed it had been a long time coming, but he figured in this life sometimes you take what you can get.

The downside was Ginger had predicted Kitty would accept, and that meant the investigation was ongoing. He was convinced it was of no consequence. Kitty would never go up to a hotel room after dinner with a married man. About that he had no doubt. She would decline, discretely and politely, and the matter would be settled. But he looked forward to dinner and drinks with a pretty nineteen-year-old cutting champion. It occurred to him the mischievous letter that had so upset his life these past few days might prove a good thing after all.

— v —

Ed called his wife on Tuesday afternoon to say he would be home late because he was meeting Bobby Dosher to make an offer on Bambam. A little before four o'clock, P.D. Rabbit messenger service delivered an oversized, lightweight pink box to Ed's office. It was wrapped with ribbon and emblazoned with the Cowgirl Couture logo. Ed left the office with it a little after five and checked into the hotel room he had reserved at Buena Hacienda. There was a bottle of scotch and two glasses on the nightstand as he had requested. He placed the Couture box on the bed and stepped back to inspect the room. Buena Hacienda was an elegant establishment with first-class accommodations, and the impressive pink box festooned with ribbons dominated the room. It seemed almost a shame Kitty would not come up here to see this.

It was early, so Ed permitted himself to relax in a plush chair and absorb the ambiance. He decided to impress Kitty by arriving fashionably late, perhaps ten after seven. He did not want to look too anxious. The scotch on the nightstand was a tempting antidote to his slight case of nerves, but Ed resolved not to touch it. He was not going to show up with alcohol on his breath.

At ten minutes after seven he rose from the chair, took a deep breath, and walked with quiet confidence into Buena Hacienda's elegant and dimly lit dining room.

"The lady hasn't arrived yet," the Maître d' told him. "I'll show you to your table."

Ed was a little unsettled but allowed himself to be seated. He studied the menu. She had still not arrived at seven-twenty. He did not allow himself to panic, or imagine she might not come, but did order a scotch from the waiter. By seven-thirty-five, he had killed the drink and ordered a second. Kitty arrived, flustered and apologetic, at seven-forty.

"My God, you're still here! Ed, I'm so sorry!" she said. "It was really busy tonight, and one of the girls was sick." She was underdressed for the occasion in a ripped and faded pair of old jeans, over which she had thrown an oversized T-shirt that probably belonged to a boyfriend, and was wearing flip-flops in the dining room.

"No, no!" he said. "I've been relaxing with a drink. I didn't even notice the time." He was hugely relieved she had not stood him up, and waved her into the other chair. "Let's get you fixed up with a drink and then you can look over the menu."

"I'll just have a lemonade," she told the waiter. Kitty

flopped into her chair, glanced over the menu, and set it aside. "Ed, you're going to hate me, but I'm supposed to meet my boyfriend at nine and he gets really upset if I'm late. Is it okay if you sort of give me the bottom line and we can do the rest of this later?"

"Oh, sure! No problem." Ed's crestfallen look betrayed him, but she did not notice.

"I've never eaten here but it's supposed to be really good," she said, glancing wistfully over the menu.

"I'll make it short so you can run," Ed said. "Ginger wants to encourage more young people to enter the sport, and decided our Amateur champion should be princess of the barbecue. She picked out some really nice high-end couture for you to wear."

Kitty looked at him in disbelief. "Seriously? Wow, I don't know what to say. Ed, that's … just wow. Is this a secret or can I tell anybody?"

"I don't suppose it's a secret now," Ed said, delighted with her sparkling eyes. "She had to guess your size, so she does want you to try on the things she picked out."

"I can't wait to see them!"

"Actually they're in a room upstairs, but I realize you have to run. We can do it another time."

"They're here? Let's do it now! It won't take a minute!"

Kitty left her lemonade on the table, and Ed reluctantly abandoned the half-finished scotch. He had not expected Kitty to be so eager, and was relieved that no one was in the hallway to see them go to the room. Ed was so nervous his hand got caught in his pocket when he tried to remove the room card. He struggled and almost ripped out his pants pocket, but finally retrieved the card and swung the door open. Kitty pushed past him into the room. She gave a little cry of excitement at the large pink box on the bed and tore it open. She did not even notice the bottle of scotch on the nightstand.

Ed quietly shut the door and watched in awe. Kitty held up a powder blue lace bandeau with shoulder strap and a white pencil skirt. "Ed, these are awesome!" she said. "They're so beautiful, and the colors are perfect! I want to try them on."

"You can change in the bathroom if you like," he suggested.

"No, it's fine," she said. Kitty pulled off her oversized T-shirt and threw it on the bed. She was wearing a shiny jet-black satin brassiere, and stepped over to the dresser to hold the powder blue bandeau over it.

Like most young people, Kitty trusted mature adults and believed them experienced with the world. She imagined a man Ed's age must have seen about a million girls in their underwear. She was as comfortable doing the fitting with him as she was disrobing for a doctor.

"This might be a little small."

While Kitty struggled to get into the bandeau, Ed edged closer to the nightstand and quietly poured half a glass of scotch. She gave up halfway. "Nope. Do you think Ginger can find it in a half size larger?"

"I'm sure it won't be a problem," Ed said, in a choked whisper.

Kitty threw the bandeau on the bed and considered the white pencil skirt. Then, to Ed's surprise, she kicked off her flip-flops and slid down and pushed away her faded jeans. She returned to the mirror in matching jet-black bra and panties, and held the white pencil skirt in front of her.

"Uh-oh. I think this is small, too."

She stepped into it and wrestled to pull it up.

Ed took a sip of scotch, staring at the sun-tanned teenager in a black satin bra and matching panties. He was learning a lot about women just as Ginger had predicted. One mystery he'd always wondered about was why pretty young girls kicked around in sloppy T-shirts over ripped and faded jeans. He now realized they did it to save money so they could buy expensive underthings to wear for their boyfriends.

Kitty managed to get into the skirt, but could only zip it up halfway.

"Can you ask Ginger if this comes a size larger?"

"I'll let her know," he said.

"Oh, the zipper's stuck." She grappled to push down the skirt.

"Let me help with that." He was starting to feel uncomfortable in a hotel room with a teenaged girl in underwear. Eager to extricate himself from the situation,

Ed set down his scotch and came up behind Kitty to free the zipper. It wouldn't move.

"It's jammed," she said.

"No, I can get it." He pushed and pulled to no avail.

"That's not helping. Let me do it."

Ed became flustered and began to attack the zipper, yanking it upward so hard Kitty was almost lifted off her feet, and then pulling it down hard again.

"Mr. Hawn, I said I'll do it!" She swatted back at him with an arm in annoyance.

Overwhelmed by a rush of panic, Ed threw his arms around her waist, swept her off her feet, and plopped her facedown on the bed. Then he climbed on her and, gripping the damned zipper with both hands, ripped it apart, splitting the skirt down its length. Kitty reached back and swatted at him again, causing him to lose balance and topple off the bed. She kicked away the skirt and sprang for the door. Ed came to his senses and scrambled after her. She unlocked the door and pulled it open, but he was upon her and slammed it shut again.

"You can't go running down the hall like that," he said. "People will get the wrong impression!"

"I want out of here!" Kitty shouted and slapped her hand at the door. "Somebody open this door! Hello?! Is anybody there?"

Almost immediately there was a loud thump as a large person threw himself against the door from outside. With the second attempt the door flew open, throwing Kitty and Ed backward. A large man who looked like an ex-Marine in a business suit entered, followed by the desk clerk.

The man held up his smartphone and was taking flash pictures. Kitty gaped wide-eyed in bra and panties, her long dark hair tousled and covering half her face. Ed stood behind her with his suit disheveled, necktie loose, and shirttail hanging outside his pants.

Ed stared. "Who are you?" he said. "This is a private room! You can't come barging in here."

The man showed identification. "Thomas Blasingame, Edwards Investigations," he said. "Your wife hired us to run surveillance on you."

"Patsy did?" Ed blinked in bewilderment.

"She said you've been acting strange lately."

"How did you find out about this room?"

"We have arrangements with employees of most hotels in the county and routinely update them on our surveillance list. We knew about this room two hours after you booked it."

Ed was aghast. The desk clerk shrugged helplessly.

"Will somebody please tell me what's going on?" Kitty demanded.

"Are you Bambam?" the detective asked.

"No, I most certainly am not!"

"Mr. Hawn told his wife he was going to look at a horse tonight."

"Okay, I'm out of here," Kitty said. She walked back

to the bed, slipped into her jeans, pulled on the T-shirt, and stepped into her flip-flops. She sailed past the men and out of the room with a furious look on her face.

Ed looked shaken as he reached for his wallet. "Mr. Blasingame," he said, "I don't know how much my wife is paying you, but I'll double it."

"I can't take money from you," Blasingame said. "It wouldn't be ethical."

"We can talk about ethics in church," Ed said. "If these pictures get out, it will ruin me."

"Your wife signed a contract and gave us a retainer. It would be a breach of fiduciary duty to take money from you. The company could get hit with one hell of a lawsuit and I'd lose my license."

"There must be something we can work out." Ed looked desperate.

Blasingame placed a reassuring hand on Ed's shoulder. "Mr. Hawn, I know this looks bad now, but it will pass. Believe me, it's very common. I see this sort of thing every day. Civilization wouldn't survive if people couldn't get through situations like this."

Ed looked helpless. The desk clerk was examining the door to see how much damage it had suffered.

— vi —

The place to look for young cowgirls on a lazy afternoon in San Bernardino County is Madelyn Wooster's Peaches

Hair Salon near Ramone. Twenty-four-year-old Andi Wilkerson, a PCCHA Non-Pro Top Ten finisher four years running, is a stylist who rents a chair from Madelyn there. Usually you will find two or three high school teens who ride Amateur hanging out in their sloppy T-shirts over ripped and faded jeans, flipping through the latest hair style or fashion magazines. It's the place to go to talk horses or kick around local gossip.

One Monday in late November Emily Hanks was in Andi's chair getting her bob trimmed, while Nicola Stanley, Zoe Cullen, and Kaylee Shepard were looking through magazines. The topic of the hour was CutAway's first annual awards barbecue the previous Sunday on Ginger's ranch. Amateur champion Mia Coalson had reigned as princess of the barbecue. Everyone said the seventeen-year-old's cropped black hair, pale skin, and dark red lipstick perfectly complimented the powder blue bandeau and white pencil skirt Ginger Witt had donated for the occasion. *Quarter Horse News* covered the affair and the reporter was said to have been so smitten with the rising young champion that Mia was under consideration for the cover.

Conspicuous by her absence was second-place winner and high school sophomore Gretchen Tankersley. When Kitty Trotka, despite a seemingly unbeatable lock on Amateur, abruptly withdrew from the competition and left town, Tankersly inherited the lead. But poor Gretchen lost her hat on a run, and when she tried to catch it, fell off her horse for an automatic sixty. That and some bad cows gave Mia the air to steal first place. Gretchen was notorious for her difficult temperament, and nobody was particularly surprised when she declined to attend to accept second place.

From there the discussion at Peaches Salon naturally drifted to a revisiting of the infamous "shit storm," as Ginger called it, that blindsided CutAway the previous August. The particulars of what exactly happened remained something of a mystery, though Ed Hawn's wife was so upset she posted the photo that quickly went viral on social media. Patsy for sure had put it out there for the world to see - Kitty Trotka in her underwear in a Buena Hacienda hotel room, glaring furiously through a tangle of dark hair, with a disheveled and unhappy-looking Ed Hawn behind her.

"Kitty looked smoking hot, to be honest," Zoe Cullen said.

"The expression on that girl's face was to die for," Em said.

"Her hair was amazing," Zoe said."Andi, I want you to make me look like that."

Andi laughed. "I can do the cut, but you'll have to figure out the rest yourself."

"I'd pay a million dollars for somebody to put a picture of me out there like that," Kaylee said wistfully.

"I want to know where she got that lingerie," Nicola said. "I can't find it anywhere."

"It might be La Senza," Zoe said.

"More like Coco de Mer to me," Kaylee said.

"Whatever," said Em. "She has the body to sell it."

"If I was her, I'd roll that kind of exposure into a modeling career," Kaylee said.

"Totally," said Zoe, flipping the page of a magazine. "Really sad she wasted that. Lightning only strikes once."

"Have you run into her lately?" Em asked Andi, who did a lot of hauling.

"I think she's still in Paso Robles," Andi said. "She was waitressing at Bistro Laurenta and doing really well the last time we talked. She rides Non-Pro now and has a new boyfriend. They're going to be hauling together. Personally, I'd say she's a lot better off now. People know a lot more about horses up there. I want to move there when I can afford it."

"Whatever happened to Ed Hawn?" Kaylee asked. "You don't see him around anymore."

"He has a hotel room down the street from his office," Zoe said. "I saw him walking to work the other day."

"Patsy's divorcing his ass," Nicola added, discarding one magazine and looking for another.

"It's really strange that you have this big story and nobody knows any details," Kaylee said.

"Nope, and they're not gonna," Andi said. She was blow-drying Emily's bob now. "Ed won't say a word. Patsy posted that picture and shut up. Kitty sure won't talk about it. I'm pretty certain Ginger knows more than she's telling, but all she'll say is it was a shit storm."

"The weird part is it happened in August," Em said. "Just like Ginger always says. I never took her seriously, but now I guess you have to wonder."

Andi laughed. Madelyn Wooster was older than the girls, and she was cutting the hair of one of her own regulars at the other end of the shop.

"Hey, Maddie," Andi called. "You've been around. These girls want to know if Ginger is right."

Listening to young women trying to figure out life reminded Maddie of how dumb she had been herself at that age. "Men cheat in August because it's August," she told them. "When it's September, they cheat because it's September."

WHISKEY CREEK

Gus Harlan sat on the edge of the dry creek under a starry sky with a half pint of whiskey. He could not get to sleep for the life of him. For several hours he had tossed fitfully with terrible night sweats in a sleeping bag under the cottonwood. Finally he gave up and got the bottle from a grocery bag under the tree, and sat on the edge of the creek to think.

Misty grazed peacefully in the cool night air. She had taken to Gus from the day he picked her out as a filly, and was allowed free reign in open pasture because she would never wander far from him. The moon was up in the east with its crescent pointing to where the sun would follow in a few hours.

Gus had been living under the cottonwood for several weeks now. The dry creek bed several feet below where he sat was littered with empty whiskey bottles. He did not know what he was going to do next.

One thought that occurred to him was to contact his

daughter, who worked as a registered nurse in a small clinic in San Luis Obispo. But Krista had broken off all contact with him, and they had not spoken for years. She did not even invite him to her wedding. He was not allowed into her house to see his own grandchild. If somebody suggested that she was too hard on her father she would say,"I think it's sad if you've gotten involved with him. I'm sorry, but I just can't do that anymore. I have a husband and child, and need to look after myself so I can take care of them. Besides, I do not know that man. He was never any kind of daddy that I can speak of. I would get so scared when he said mean things to my mother that made her cry, and then she would start breaking stuff. We're not even related as far as I'm concerned."

Krista was a lot different from her mother. Iona had gone girl crazy over Gus the moment they met. He chanced on her at a friend's house where he had gone to watch a football game. They connected like a clean pool shot. He remembered the night he was taking her to a foreign art movie and she had him pull over at a liquor store. She bought a couple of canned margaritas and put them away in her purse. Then, before getting back in the car, she slipped out of her panties and dropped them in the purse with the margaritas. Those were wild days, and she had been girl crazy over him for many years.

When his booze troubles first started, she went to AA meetings with him and they got through it together. That worked for a while. But somehow as he got older, Gus would become more easily fed up with things, or just tired of everything in general, and want to be left alone so he could put away a few.

Over the years he made a pretty good living for his family as a small independent contractor. He was well-liked, quick with a funny story, and always willing to help out the other fellow in a pinch. The first few times he tripped up on booze, people said it was no more his fault than a railroad crossing accident. They said a snake had crawled up his pants, but he would shake it out and get things back together.

Eventually Iona was no longer willing to go to AA with him. Friends jumped in to pick up the slack at first, and when they tailed off it fell to his sponsor to come looking for him. "If you feel like you want to drink that's fine, Gus," he would say. "All I ask is that you shoot me a dingle first so we can talk about it." Gus quickly learned to ditch this aggravating nuisance.

He was half through the bottle now, and the whiskey and night air began to have a calming effect on him. While flailing about in the sleeping bag with night sweats he had been frightened to death about what was to become of him. Now, sitting by the creek with the half pint of whiskey, he felt a little foolish for letting himself get so excited. Misty was still grazing peacefully in the dim moonlight not far away, and he realized nothing bad was about to happen.

Gus knew he had been on a pretty good run for some time now and that it had cost him his wife and his property. But now that fear had loosened its grip, he realized it was not the end of the world. Nobody had died or anything. Though he had never taken things quite this far before, he had always managed to pull them back together somehow.

Gus wanted things to go back to the way they used to be. He wished he could chuck this last bottle into the creek and then take Misty back to town and pick up his old life again. People might cut him some slack. On second thought, he had to admit they had probably already cut him his fair share. They were still nice enough, and would always help out with Misty, but otherwise had pretty much moved on with their lives. Probably he had burned them out.

Iona was a different matter, though. They had been a big part of each other's lives for many years. The house where they had raised their daughter was still there on the edge of town. Iona was probably at home sleeping in it right now. This was only a few miles from where he sat, though he was not allowed to cross the property line due to a restraining order.

Gus wondered if he could maybe just get to his feet and go home right now like nothing had happened. He was tired of living this way and wanted to sleep in his own house again. He wanted to nestle in bed with his wife again, too. He longed to slip an arm around her while she slept, and snuggle close to feel her breathing against his chest, and smell her hair in his face. He would feel safe and not have to be afraid for a while, and would fall into a deep restful sleep, the likes of which he had not known for a long time. He wished he could do that right now. It passed his mind that she would be asleep now, and he might could slip into bed without her noticing. He would sneak out again at daybreak and be gone before she woke up. He would not bother her during the day.

Sitting by the creek under the stars with the whiskey, he began to study the idea more seriously. He did not want her to wake up and catch him in bed. He would have to knock on the door and wake her up, and see if she would permit this. It wasn't asking all that much when you considered how many years they had shared. He would need to explain it right. He wasn't sure how to do that but felt it would come to him when she opened the door. He could see her looking up at him with those big blue eyes, sleepy and confused about what he wanted out there so late. But she would listen while he spoke, and would see in his face that he was sincere and meant every word. She might have to think a moment. But he could see her nod and say, "Well, if it's so important to you, I guess, whatever…," and swing open the door. If she did that his world would fall back into place again.

Gus decided to saddle up Misty and go ask Iona while he was sure about this. He capped the whiskey but was a little unsteady getting to his feet. It was a struggle to throw the saddle on Misty, and by the time he got it cinched, he was too worn out to pull himself into it. He had to sit and rest a minute, but decided not to uncap the whiskey. Once he had passed out and tumbled into the creek, and woke up among the litter of bottles the next day. He did not want that to happen now. Misty came up from behind and nibbled at him affectionately while he watched the silent night stars. Shortly he got to his feet, and this time was able to pull himself into the saddle.

Misty knew how to get there once she figured out where he wanted to go. They owned a three bedroom wood frame house on unincorporated land just outside the Atascadero city limits. There was a four-horse barn with paddock in the rear and a few acres of pasture beyond that. It was on an unpaved road with shade trees, a neighbor across the street, and a few more houses nearby.

The place was dark and quiet. Somebody's car was parked behind Iona's in the driveway. Gus pulled up Misty at the property line and studied the situation. He did not recognize the car and had not expected this complication. He uncapped the whiskey and took a shot while he pondered this. He concluded that he would be unable to sleep until he found out what she had to say, but was reluctant to cross the property line.

"Iona!" he called toward the house.

There was only silence.

He walked Misty along the road to another part of the

property line and tried again. "Iona, are you there? Come outside a minute. I need to talk to you."

He turned Misty and walked her back along the property line. "Hello? Please, Iona! This is important."

The house remained silent. Misty had all the patience in the world, content to be with Gus wherever he was. But he had had enough.

"Goddamn it!" he swore at the still night air.

Gus knocked back the last of the whiskey and flung the bottle at the house. It smashed through a front window and shattered glass into the living room. He looked to see what would happen next. Eventually a light came on somewhere in the house.

"Iona?"

Alex Presser peered out the front door in a pair of boxer shorts. He was a young clerk at the feed store where Iona worked as bookkeeper.

"Beat it, Gus," he shouted. "She doesn't want to see you."

"Son of a bitch. What are you doing in my house, Alex?"

"None of your business. Get out of here."

"Pissant little feed store clerk. You never even finished high school."

"You need to blow before the sheriff comes and locks you up."

"Nothing you loaded in my pickup was ever right. You could fuck up a peanut butter sandwich."

"I mean it, Gus. Don't even think about crossing that property line."

That was too much for Gus. He nudged Misty forward across the ditch and onto the front lawn.

"Go tell Iona I said to get her ass out here now."

"You sorry old sot. Everybody else might feel sorry for you, but I don't. I'll beat the hell out of you right now, if that's what you want."

"Hey, I've got a surprise for you."

Gus dismounted and began to open the satchel where he kept a pistol for self-defense.

"Don't try something crazy. I know where she keeps the shotgun."

"I got six hollow points you can have."

"If somebody gets killed tonight it won't be me."

Gus found the pistol and released the safety catch. Alex swore and disappeared into the house. Gus waited to see what he was going to do. Alex returned with a shotgun.

"I paid for every dime of this place," Gus shouted. "I want you off my property."

"I'll kill you right now, Gus. I'll blow you clear across the street."

Iona appeared in the doorway behind Alex. She was wrapped in a housecoat and had her hair pinned up for sleep. "Oh crap," she said. "Alex, I told you to make him go away, not shoot him!"

"Damn bastard pulled a weapon on me."

"This is bullshit!" she yelled. "You two morons are raising a shit storm out here in the middle of the night! This is a decent neighborhood and people are trying to sleep. The whole world's going to know about it tomorrow. I'll be too embarrassed to show my face!"

"Go back in the house, Iona," Alex ordered her. "I've got this."

"Oh screw you, mister feed store clerk! Did I give you permission to get that? Put it down right now!"

Alex saw she meant it. Sullenly he lowered the weapon, keeping a wary eye on Gus.

She turned on him next. "Gus Harlan, have you lost your mind? You're in violation of a court order! The judge told you not to come anywhere near this property."

A porch light came on somewhere across the street.

"Iona, I need to ask you something. It's important. Please talk to me."

He was a pitiful sight. "If you want to say something to me, you need to put that pistol away first."

Gus had forgotten he was holding it, and looked almost surprised to see it in his hand. He did like she said and went to put it back in the satchel.

"I don't want you talking to him, Iona."

"Oh shut up, Alex. Put that shotgun back where you found it. Don't you dare do something like that without asking me." Alex reluctantly started back inside. "I think there's still some scotch left in that bottle," she called after him. "Bring it out here."

Gus had not seen Iona in a long time, and the sight of her took the fight out of him. He was grateful to see her but frightened that she was so angry with him.

"Okay, now you can talk to me. Come over here and tell me what's so important you had to wake up the whole damn neighborhood."

Gus was no longer confident it had been a good idea to come here. He was not even sure if he was steady enough to make it across the grass to where she stood on the porch. But he realized this was probably his last chance to say anything to her. It was too late to turn back now. Iona watched with a stern expression as he shakily navigated the lawn to where she waited.

"Now what's so important you had to wake up the whole neighborhood in the middle of the night?"

His mind raced for the right words to express the feelings that had overwhelmed him at the creek.

"We spent a lot of years together in this house," he began, but the thought trailed away.

"That's right, Gus. What about it?"

Gus was silent. His mind was scrambling all over the lot for the right words but could not come up with much.

"I used to sleep next to you ... in the bed in there..."

"Go on. I'm really interested to see where you're going with this."

Alex returned with the half bottle of scotch and watched. Gus hesitated, and then the words tumbled out. "Sometimes I would put my arm around you and feel you breathing against me, and smell your hair in my face."

Alex snorted. Iona shot him a hard look.

"Gus, if you want to ask me something, you'd better take your shot now."

"I need some rest in the worst way, Iona," he blurted suddenly. "I want to come inside and sleep next to you for a little while."

She looked at him.

"I really need to do that. Please, Iona. I'll be gone at daylight. Nobody will ever know. If I can just get some rest maybe I can get back on my feet again. I'm a good contractor. People like my work."

"This is what you woke up the whole neighborhood to tell me? Gus, does any of that make sense to you at all? I sure hope not, because if it does I guarantee you've lost your marbles all over the sidewalk."

"I'm this close to getting it together, Iona. I'm sure of it. You'll see."

"You know you can't stay here, Gus."

It was not going like he had pictured. "Please don't make me go away, Iona," he pleaded. "I'll be good, I promise. I won't drink a drop."

"I just told you, no."

"Look, I'm going to just walk through that door and slip into our bed right now. I won't bother you a bit. You'll see."

He took a step toward her.

"Don't, Gus."

He did.

"Gus, I said no! No means no!"

Gus froze up on his feet where he stood. He could not take another step. He was busted.

"Alex, give him that bottle and put him back on Misty."

Alex did like she said. He helped Gus up onto his horse and handed up the bottle, then led Misty back onto the road and got her started. Gus looked beaten, but gripped the bottle tightly so it did not fall.

Alex retuned to the house and tried to put an arm around Iona. She threw it off. "You get a pillow and sleep on the couch," she snapped. "I don't want to be next to anybody right now."

About a half hour later Field Commander Bill Cullen and Deputy Lionel Thompson of the sheriff's department pulled up in a county vehicle with a horse trailer in tow. The place was dark so they took a look around the premises with flashlights and examined the broken window. Cullen went up on the porch and knocked. The lights came on and Iona opened the door. Alex was looking out behind her.

"I hear you had quite a ruckus out here tonight, Iona," he said. "What was that about?"

"Oh, Gus showed up drunk and wanted to sleep over. He's gone now. I'm sorry you had to come all this way. I'm so embarrassed about this."

"Son of a bitch pulled a gun on me," Alex added.

"You need to find him and let him sleep it off in jail."

"Shut up, Alex. He's gone now. He won't be back."

"Do you want to file a complaint about the window?"

"No, save yourself some trouble and leave him alone. This never happened before. He knows better than to come back."

"I'll press charges if she won't," Alex said. "I want him locked up before he kills somebody."

"Alex, butt out. This is none of your business so just shut up."

"Well, I just want to be sure you're safe," Cullen said.

"I'm fine," she told him.

Alex put a protective arm around her. "Don't worry about Iona, Sheriff," he said confidently. "I'll be here to look out for her."

She threw his arm off again. "Oh, you just want to blow somebody's head off!"

"He still staying out by the creek?"

"I suppose, but leave him alone, Bill. Don't go out there this time of night."

"Well, I need to speak to him about something else. Might as well do it now, since we're here."

"I'm sorry you had to come out so late. Be careful driving across that pasture in the dark."

Bill and Lionel went back to their vehicle. "You, back on the couch!" she told Alex as they went back inside. "I don't want you in the same bed with me right now."

Gus was sitting on the edge of the creek when Cullen

and the deputy drove up to the cottonwood. He had finished the scotch, and the bottle was down in the creek bed somewhere with the others. Misty was still saddled and bridled, waiting patiently under the cottonwood. Gus saw them pull up, but then looked off at the stars without interest.

The lawmen went over to Misty. Bill removed the pistol from the saddlebag, while Lionel ran a hand over her and saw that she was clean of infections and well-fed. Then the deputy picked up her feet to look them over. "She's well shod and took care of down here." Bill removed the bridle and checked her tongue. "Mouth is clean." Lionel pulled off the saddle and ran a hand over her back looking for sores. "We've got a sound animal here, sir."

"She looks pretty quiet," Bill said. "See if you can load her."

Lionel started putting a halter on her. Bill walked over to the creek to talk to Gus.

Gus sat on the edge of the drop above the clutter of bottles, looking up at the stars. The two men had gone to high school together but that was a long time ago.

"Hello, Gus."

Gus looked back at him with an uncertain expression.

"Am I going to jail?" he asked weakly.

"Do what...? Oh, no no. Hell, I wouldn't put you in jail, Gus. We just came by to see how you're doing is all."

"I'm all right."

"That's good, I'm glad to hear that. Listen, we brought you a few groceries. Lionel's going to put them under the tree for you."

Gus understood and nodded appreciation.

Bill removed a paper from his jacket pocket. "Look, I need to talk to you about this HFA thing."

"Who…?"

"Those Humans For Animals people. I guess somebody said something to them, because they filed a complaint against you. Don't you remember I had to serve you?"

"Complaint about what…?"

"Well, they say you're unfit to possess an animal companion."

"Tell 'em to go jump in this creek. I take good care of Misty. She's fine."

"The thing is, a judge has issued a court order."

"For what? I didn't do anything."

"It says I have to take her."

Gus looked at him like he was talking crazy.

"Why? They can't do that."

"Goddamn it, Gus. You never showed up!"

Gus looked at him blankly.

"I did what…?"

"You defaulted! There's no way in hell the HFA could have won this thing. All you had to do was contest it. Now look what you've done to me. I'm the son of a bitch who has to execute the judgment. Do you think I like this? Why in the hell did you do this to me?"

"I showed up…" Gus said weakly.

"Well they sure couldn't find you."

"I must have been there somewhere…"

"Oh hell, you don't know what's real and what's not anymore. Don't you remember when I served you? I gave you that piece of paper and explained the whole thing. You told me that you would take care of it. That's all you had to do."

"I might be messed up on some things, but I would never let anything bad happen to Misty. Ask Lori Summers. She's still Misty's vet even though I can't pay her right now. Talk to Joe Eberle. He shods her for nothing. Gov Lengel gives me supplements from his feed store. Old man Ratliff says she can pasture out here for as long as I need to. Talk to them, Bill. They'll tell you what a sound animal I've got."

"They needed to let the judge hear that. Lori Summers would have testified for you. Joe Eberle would have been there. Hell, we all would have showed up. All you had to do was ask. Nobody knew anything about this until a paper landed on my desk, and now I have to execute it."

"Tell 'em where to stick it."

"It's not like that. I'm a sworn officer of the law. I have to carry out a legal court order. That's the way it is."

"You're going to take her…?"

"I have to now!"

"Please don't do that, Bill. Don't take Misty. I need

her. She's real important to me right now."

"I don't have a choice!"

"Tell them you couldn't find me. We'll stay out of sight somewhere."

"It's too late for that. This is what we're looking at."

He gave the paper to Gus, and went back to help Lionel get Misty in the trailer. The deputy had a halter on her now, and she loaded without any trouble. Then they got two large sacks of groceries from the truck and set them against the tree.

Bill went back to where Gus sat by the creek.

"If you want to say goodbye, now would be the time."

Gus did not feel like he could get to his feet right now. He did not see much point in attempting it anyway. He had become accustomed to things disappearing on him by now. Once something went away on him, he knew it would not be back.

He shook his head. "No, that's all right," he said.

Gus turned away and looked at the starry sky.

Bill waited for a moment to make sure this was how it was going to end. Finally he sighed and leaned down and whispered to Gus.

"God help me, but I slipped a bottle in those groceries for you."

Gus heard him and just nodded quietly.

"I can't tell you what to do with it. I wish you'd pour it down a rat hole somewhere or out on the ground, and throw the empty down in the creek with the others. But I guess you know what's best for you by now."

Gus looked away at the sky and did not answer. Bill left him there and went back to the truck. He and Lionel pulled away with Misty.

A little after they left Gus got to his feet and made his way to the cottonwood. He found the bottle and brought it back to the creek to sit and think. The whiskey helped him to not have to accept that Misty was gone from his life now too. The sun would be up before long, and he intended to crawl into his sleeping bag and get some rest. He had no idea what to do next. It occurred to him that if he slept through the day, he would feel better in the evening, and something might come to him.

WIDE RIVER

"The horse doesn't feel a thing," Steve Willit said. "They position the captive bolt gun right about here." He placed two fingers to his forehead above his eyes. "The bolt fires directly into the brain. Activists like to post videos of horses thrashing around. You're just looking at a carcass. The horse is gone. It's like a chicken flopping around after its head is chopped off."

We were eating breakfast in a booth at Josie's, a little café on the west side of town where he had agreed to meet me. It was the summer of my first year at Oklahoma University, and I had stayed over in Norman for a great literature seminar taught by a famous visiting professor. I was in need of pocket money, but with the country in recession there wasn't a whole lot out there. Somebody in a hardware store told me to talk to Willit. He was a local farrier and cutting horse competitor who owned a ranch somewhere out near Lawton, I believe. I couldn't imagine what he might have for me but called anyway.

He said a young college student might be someone he could work with and suggested we meet. Josie's was about half-way between us, though I now think he picked it because neither of us was likely to come across anyone we knew there.

I liked Steve Willit a lot. He was raising two little girls out on the ranch with his wife, Rebecca, and seemed decent and knowledgeable. I was only a year out of high school but he treated me like an equal. We shared thoughts about what we wanted out of life, and by the time we finished breakfast felt comfortable with each other.

Like most people in the horse business, he had to know a lot about markets and the economy. Real estate had collapsed a couple of years back, and he explained how that had tripped-up not just him but a lot of other ranchers and trainers.

"Greed is what's killing the horses," he said. "I can't tell you how frustrating that is to people like me who are in the business." He talked a little about breeders registering too many foals and then dumping their failures on an already saturated domestic pet market. But he really got rolling when he started in on the big banks, and how they had triggered the collapse in real estate that had thrown the country into such a bad recession.

It seemed to me horsemen were about the savviest people you could ask about how capital flow and markets are connected. The way Steve explained it, a ten-year housing bubble had been fueled by sub-par mortgages issued by greedy banks. All that lending to unqualified buyers increased the default rate on mortgages. Mortgage-based financial products began to underperform and investors stopped buying them. Investment houses were stuck with a backlog of inventory and quit buying home mortgages. Banks now had so much capitol tied up in mortgages they were short on cash to perform other services.

"Leslie, you go to college, so I'm pretty sure you can follow this," Steve said. "Suppose a retailer in San Francisco needs a letter of credit so a manufacturer in China can ship him toys for the Christmas season. If the bank is deep into mortgages, it won't have cash reserves to issue the letter of credit. The retailer has a poor Christmas without toys to sell while the manufacturer's warehouse is overstocked with product. Retailers lay off sales clerks and manufacturers lay off workers. Unemployment goes up and pushes even more people into default on home mortgages. We still haven't seen the bottom of this thing."

What he said made a lot of sense, though I didn't quite understand how so many people in high government or corporate positions could have allowed it to happen.

Steve said the horse industry had been among the first to feel the hit because it was particularly sensitive to economic weakness. The day when the horse was a necessity is long past, was how he explained it. There are still a lot of people out there who would love to own one. But even if horses were free, few people could afford the expense of upkeep. It is not a dog or cat. You're talking stable fees, farrier bills, vet bills, trailers, stall maintenance, and I can't even imagine what else he left out.

Anytime the economy slows, people have to cut back on nonessentials. If it goes into crisis, they start shedding horses like a dog shaking off fleas. Steve's farrier business was losing clients, and he couldn't pick up the slack by selling off his own horses because everyone else was getting rid of them, too.

"Things are so bad I've caught people trying to sneak their horses onto my property at night and leave them for me to look after. Ask any rancher, he'll tell you the same thing. They have to police horse auctions now to keep animals from being abandoned there. We're seeing horses turned loose in open country to fend for themselves. What in God's name is wrong with somebody who would do that? I'm pretty sure he's hard up and probably in foreclosure, but what makes him think somebody else is going to look after his animals? Nobody else can afford them either."

Steve leaned back in the booth and gathered his thoughts. When he sat forward again, he spoke in a more confidential tone. "Nobody wants to hear this part," he said, "but where do you think all those horses end up? We banned slaughterhouses in this country, but trailers are rolling day and night, hauling excess horses to Canada and Mexico. That's just how it is right now and there's nothing anybody can do to stop it."

Steve seemed satisfied he could trust me, but continued in a low voice so no one else could overhear.

"Leslie, I know a young student like you can always use a little extra money," he said. "God knows I sure can. Now, there are a lot of people out there who need to let go of their horses, and one way or another, most of them are going to end up with kill buyers. We can't help that, but I believe we can make a little money off it without hurting anybody." He paused to see if he had lost me. I was still listening but felt out of my depth. "If what I'm about to say doesn't feel right to you," he said, "I'll pick up the breakfast tab and let's walk out of here and forget we ever met. But I'm looking for a nice young fellow like you. I believe we can help each other out."

I was impressed with Steve Willit and wanted to work with him. I wasn't sure where he was going with this, but told him I was open to learning something new as long as it was legal.

"Son, I would never drag you into something against the law," he said. "I'm talking about an opportunity to help people who can't afford to keep their horses, by relieving them of concern the animal will end up with a kill buyer. If we can do that and get paid for it, would it interest you?"

I said it might, but felt something wasn't right. I was

away from home and on my own for the first time and eager to learn new things. Steve made me feel like an adult, but I sensed my parents would not approve of me getting into something I was too inexperienced to understand.

"Being in the farrier business, I pretty much know who needs to get rid of a horse around here," he said. "They are scared to death their animals will end up in a slaughterhouse, and will pretty much give them away to the right person to avoid that. Now, let me be honest about this. One way or another, most of these horses are going to Mexico. That's the economic reality right now. Nobody wants to talk about it, but anybody with his head screwed on right knows it. We can't change that, but we can help out folks who need to let go of their livestock. I believe that's a good thing under the circumstances, and we can improve ourselves financially doing it."

I was pretty sure my mother would not allow me to get involved with Steve Willit if we were in Beaumont. She had been pretty strict about girls and other things we disagreed on back home, and generally got her way. But I was on my own in Oklahoma now and would have to figure this one out for myself. Though something about it didn't feel right, everything Steve Willit said made sense.

Steve took my silence to mean I was still in play. He showed me some glossy business cards for an organization called Milton's Meadows Horse Refuge.

"A fellow named Dominic Henstill owns this property," he said. "You can check out his website. Milton's Meadows pledges any horse donated to the refuge will be sheltered and well cared for while they make a good faith effort to place it in a proper home. Now, I can tip you off on who to contact about donating an animal to them. Believe me, people are going to be thrilled to find a young college student who is doing summer volunteer work for a refuge, and who offers to take a horse off their hands."

I fingered the business card, trying to figure this out. "Why can't you give them this card yourself?"

"Leslie, I like to think I'm a good person. People around here know me. I have a family and reputation to protect, and can't risk having my name involved in this. But let me be straight with you. There's not enough refuge acreage in the whole country to accept ten percent of the excess horses out there. Henstill is a kill buyer for an operation in Mexico. He opened this refuge to siphon off excess horses from people who need to sell, but are afraid the animal will go to a kill buyer."

"Is that legal?" I was still awash.

"Milton's Meadows delivers one hundred percent on the terms of the transfer-of-ownership contract," Steve said. "They pledge to make a good faith effort to place donated horses in good homes. Everybody knows that's not going to happen in this market. But the attempt fulfills the obligation, and then he can dispose of the horse. That's how it works in the real world. People might not admit it, but there are times when they don't want the truth. They want somebody to tell them what they need to hear. These people are suffering from a world of hurt, and need a way to do what they have to do and not feel bad about it. We don't take a dime from them. They donate the animal to Milton's Meadows. Henstill sells it to the slaughterhouse and we get a commission check for the referral. Our money comes from Mexico."

I studied the card again. "You'll tell me who to contact, but otherwise we don't know each other?"

Steve nodded. "This meeting never happened," he said. "If this thing were to unravel and it came out I was involved with Henstill, my farrier business and ranching operation would be ruined. It's different with you. You're from out of state, and you're going to graduate and move on, anyway."

Steve slid a slip of paper across the table to me. "This man needs to sell yesterday. You ought to call him and see how it goes. Tell him you're a student volunteer and ask to see the horse. Then give him a card and suggest he contact them. That's it. You'll never see him again. Henstill's people will handle the paperwork and pick up the horse. We split the commission check down the middle."

I studied the name on the slip of paper. "I'd like to think about this," I said.

"It's entirely up to you, son. I hope you give it a try. Nobody will get hurt. If it doesn't feel right, you can walk away and no hard feelings. But I believe we can make money together."

— ii —

Steve left me with a lot to consider back in my off campus summer apartment. A graduate history student who had been my TA was having me house-sit his place while he was in Australia; I looked after his cat, Mr. Pink, and drove his car enough so the battery wouldn't die.

My folks wanted me to come home to Beaumont, but I was relishing my new independence. The past year had been a heady experience, on my own in the world for the first time without the folks looking over my shoulder to decide things for me.

I lay on the bed with the orange tabby purring on my chest and considered the slip of paper Steve had given me. Mr. Pink sniffed at it, though it wasn't anything for him. A fellow named Robert Holm needed to find a new owner for a horse called Posey. I wondered who this man was, and what he might be like, and what sort of circumstances had put him in such crisis. Steve said the man would be grateful to hear from me. I wasn't at all sure I wanted to get involved in this, but was intrigued enough that I did not see the harm in making the call.

An older man answered.

"Yes, sir," I said. "I'm calling to see if the horse you advertised is still available."

"Well, we're still trying to find the right home for her. Where did you see our ad?"

"Horseclicks," I said. Steve had written that on the scrap of paper too. "Actually, I'm a student volunteer for Milton's Meadows Horse Refuge. There's a lot of excess horses on the market right now, and we're contacting sellers to see if they've been able to place their animals. Sometimes we're able to help out."

"What's your name, son?"

"Leslie Willbanks. I'll be a sophomore at OU this fall."

"Well, I appreciate your call, son. No, we're still hoping something will come up."

"Can you tell me a little about the horse?"

"She's a very gentle sixteen-year-old red dun mare. Fourteen hands, good health. My daughter grew up with her. We hate to let her go, but our circumstances have changed."

"Yes, there's a lot of that these days," I said. "Where is the horse now?"

"She has a paddock behind the house. We're zoned for horses out here so it's been an ideal situation. But I lost my job last year, and I've been offered a position in Atlanta. My daughter graduated high school and flies for Delta so she lives in Dallas. We'd like to keep Posey, but our house is in escrow and we just can't afford a boarding ranch right now. Annie doesn't get home much to spend time with her, anyway. My wife and I discussed this and feel we have to let her go. Posey has been family for so many years that it's been a hard decision."

"Let me ask you this," I said. "Would you be interested in donating her to an animal refuge where she would be cared for until they can place her in a good home?"

"Well, Annie's been insisting on meeting the new owner face-to-face. She wants to be sure it's someone who will love Posey as much as we do. Don't get me wrong, I know it's just a horse. But Posey and my daughter took to each other when she was growing up. We feel she's part of the family. When you've lived with an animal for that long, you hate to just throw her to the wind."

"I certainly understand that, sir," I said. "I just wanted to let you know about Milton's Meadows, because sometimes they can help people like you."

"Well, I appreciate that, son. To be honest, with the property in escrow, we're running out of options. My wife and daughter are getting a little upset about the situation. How would we go about exploring something like that?"

"Start with our website," I said. "It shows our facilities and has endorsements from people we've helped. We're mostly young volunteers like me from all over. We also have a few ranchers who have stepped forward and pledged to accept some of our animals until we can find a permanent home for them."

"It sounds like something we should think about."

"If you like, I can come by and look at the – at Posey

– to make sure she's right for our program."

He considered this for a moment. "Maybe you ought to do that, son," he said. "Let me give you our address. It would be a godsend if we qualified for something like this."

I wrote down directions to Robert Holm's house and said I would be there that afternoon.

"Leslie, I appreciate you taking the trouble to contact us," he said. "It's hard to become bitter about life when there's young people like you in the world."

I hung up and lay on the bed fiddling with my phone and mulled over how easily that had gone. This was not something I would have considered for a minute growing up in Beaumont. But I was on my own in Oklahoma now, and eager to become more sophisticated about how the real world works.

It looked to me like Steve could be right. Mr. Holm seemed grateful for the helping hand I was offering. Steve and I might not save any horses, but people count for something too, and we were not charging them a dime. Steve said our commission shaved a little profit off the kill buyers, and I couldn't see anything wrong with that. They would get the horse anyway, one way or another. We were just making it easier on the people who had to let the animal go.

I suppose everybody lies once in a while, but that was the only part I wasn't sure about. I ran what Steve had said though my mind several times, and somehow it always made sense. The only way to find out how I felt for sure was to go to see Mr. Holm.

The directions took me to a large tract of undeveloped land outside Newcastle that was being prepared for new homes when the recession brought construction to a halt. The Holms residence was a ranch-style house on a cul-de-sac in an older subdivision out there. They had a fairly new sedan and a Land Rover in the driveway. The realtor's placard on the front yard said "Sold," and I could see curtains had already been taken down from the living room windows.

I rang the bell and waited. A man and woman were talking somewhere inside. The man who opened the door was in his forties, with the benign and slightly tired look of someone who had been out of work for a while.

"Mr. Holm? Leslie Willbanks."

"Hello, son. I appreciate you coming." He opened the screen door enough to shake my hand. "Listen, my wife and I discussed this and we've decided to stay out of it. You need to talk to Annie. She's in back with one of her friends. Why don't you just go around the side of the house there. She'll introduce you to Posey and the two of you can talk."

There was a wooden gate along the side of the house. I opened the latch and passed down a narrow corridor between the house and a high hedge separating their property from the lot next door. I emerged into a dazzling sunlit backyard; it was about an acre of land,

and beyond the far fence I could see another acre of undeveloped land that ran to a distant boulevard. Except for a paddock behind the garage, it was nothing but green grass and blue sky.

Annie was saddled up on Posey, a dark-haired girl on a red dun mare, talking to a tall blonde girl in shorts stretched on a deck lounge on the veranda. The blonde was sipping iced tea from a tall glass with a slice of orange on the rim. I was struck by how lucky some girls are to grow up around horses like this, even though I sensed it was the end of something.

"Hi," the dark-haired girl said. "Are you Leslie?"

"Leslie Willbanks. Mr. Holm said I could find Annie back here."

"I'm Annie." She reached down and offered her hand. I touched it. "And this is Claire."

"Hello," Claire said. A little flick of her fingers was all I got, along with just the trace of a smile. Her blue eyes briefly swept over me with a look of curiosity. Though we were about the same age, I was a little intimidated by these girls. They were flight attendants who I imagined must have seen a lot of the world and been through several boyfriends since high school.

"Claire came up from Dallas for moral support," Annie said. She dismounted and gently pulled the horse a little closer. "And this is Posey."

I stroked Posey on the nose and she reacted as if pleased by my touch.

"She likes people," Annie said. "She's very trusting."

"I'm supposed to ask you some questions," I said. Steve had given me a list of things to ask that a horse refuge would want to know. "Is she suitable for a small child?"

"Oh, totally. I was nine when I got her."

"What about physical problems?"

"She's older, but sound. I have all her vet records."

"What's inside of her?" Steve said this was important because horses fed certain hormones or supplements might not be fit for human consumption.

"Just sunshine, water, and a healthy diet."

Claire was eating the orange slice from her tea, but I could tell she was listening to us talk.

"Do you want to ride her?" Annie said.

"Actually, I'm not exactly a horse person, to be honest."

"Oh, my God. Then what are you doing here?"

"Like I said, I'm a summer volunteer."

"Well, we can't have that," Annie said. "Okay, Posey's never killed anyone yet. Put your foot in here and grab the saddle horn." Claire was watching with interest now to see what was going to happen.

I did like Annie said and pulled myself into the saddle. Posey adjusted to my weight and I guess was sort of making up her mind about me. I got a feel for the reins.

"Now just give her a little touch with your heels and tell her to go."

We trotted down the length of the yard to the rail fence. Cars whispered down the asphalt boulevard in the distance, and you could see a new shopping center across from that. The veranda where Annie and Claire waited was about a football field away. I stroked Posey's neck with my hand. She was a fine companion, all right.

"Okay Posey, let's do this!" I said. I gave her a gentle kick and we returned at a trot to rejoin the girls.

I think Claire had been watching to see if I would fall over the fence when we pulled to a halt, and I'm sure she would have laughed about it. But I had handled everything fine and was a little pleased with myself.

"She's pretty easy, all right," I said.

I dismounted and offered Annie the reins. We were both a little unsure about the next step.

"Did you have a chance to look at our website?"

"I did. I think it's wonderful what you're doing. It's just, well, I was hoping to meet the new owner. I'd like to be sure it's someone who cares about her like we do."

"If you can find someone you feel is right for Posey, that's absolutely the way to go."

"We're trying, but it's not working."

"Why don't we do this. Give it a little more time and see if something comes up. If not, this horse is fine with us."

She took the glossy business card from me. "Is this your number?"

"No, I'm just here to screen the animal. You won't see

me again. I'll leave a copy of the transfer-of-ownership agreement to look over. If you decide to go this route, they'll send someone out to settle the paperwork and take possession. It's pretty easy."

She glanced at the transfer agreement and folded it with the business card.

"Thank you for coming all the way out here, Leslie," she said. "I have a good feeling about you. I wish you were the one taking Posey, because then I wouldn't worry about her at all. But I feel a lot better about this now."

I gave Posey's nose a little rub and said goodbye to Annie. Claire was looking for something in her purse, so I was unable to catch her eye and left without saying anything to her.

I was getting in the car to leave when someone called to me.

"Hey, college boy!" It was Claire. She had followed me and was standing by the gate at the side of the house. "Get back here! You forgot something." There was a mischievous look about her.

I went back to see what she wanted. She held up a twenty-dollar bill and then slipped it into my shirt pocket.

"What's that?"

"You ran off without your tip," she said.

"You can't do that. Nobody tips volunteers."

Then I realized by the twinkle in her eyes that she was messing with me. Claire laughed and threw her arms around me and embraced me so tightly I thought she would squeeze the breath out of me. Then she pulled back and gave me a quick peck on the cheek.

"She's going to do it!" she said. "Leslie, where do guys like you come from?" She reached up and pushed back the hair that had fallen across my face. "You have no idea how important what you just did was for Annie, do you?"

"It was nothing," I said. I was a little embarrassed that she was making such a big fuss over this. Steve said people would be grateful, but this was not exactly how I wanted to impress a girl like Claire.

"Yup, totally clueless," she said. "You don't know how wonderful you are. I'm so sick of jerks. Look, do you have a girlfriend?"

"No."

"Okay, that's it. I'm taking you to dinner, someplace really nice. No arguments."

"Dinner where?" I would not have had the courage to ask out a girl like this, and here she was all over me. I was impressed with how confident and self-assured she was about herself.

"I have to fly tomorrow but I'll call when I'm back," she said. "What's your number?"

"Fly where?" I was in a daze.

"Amsterdam. I have back-to-back turnarounds so it'll be about a week. What's your number?"

I told her and she entered it into her phone.

The next few days were a blur. I couldn't get Claire out of my head. Was she really going to call? I knew I wanted to see her again, but was a little scared about her being so impressed with the things I told Annie. I reminded myself that what I had done was for Annie's own good, but it still didn't feel right.

I called Steve that same day and told him things had gone well and I thought the Holms would go with the refuge.

"I knew I was right about you," he said.

"Look, I don't think I want to do this anymore," I said.

Steve was disappointed but respected my wishes. He said he would send my commission cut, and that I should give him a call if I changed my mind. I knew I would not. I still couldn't say whether what we had done was good or bad, but it was a world away from the person Claire had mistaken me for.

I wasn't sure if Claire would really call when she was back from Europe, but I hoped she would. I wanted to see her again, and worried that she might find someone else in Amsterdam.

— iii —

I realized Claire was my girlfriend when she started picking out underwear for me in a Nordstrom's in Dallas. We're talking twenty-five-dollar-a-pair Ralph Lauren Polo, Tommy Hilfiger, Calvin Klein. Red, blue, green, black, anything but white. When we got back to my summer apartment in Norman, she started going through the dresser and threw out all my tighty-whiteys. She said she never wanted to catch me in them again.

We had talked about moving in together. By now, Claire and I had been seeing each other all summer, and the graduate student would be back from Australia so I had to find another place. She said if we could find something off campus in Norman, she could take a shuttle flight from Will Rogers to Dallas to work her Delta flights.

I liked her a lot but struggled to hold back my feelings because I wasn't sure she was really going to stay. Claire was a year older than me, had grown up in Long Beach, and had gone to work for Delta right out of high school. She knew her way around famous cities across the world, while the OU campus was about as far as I had been from Beaumont. She was comfortable ordering in high-end restaurants, bought her bathing suits at a favorite shop in Sweden, got her electronics in Tokyo, knew how to handle getting propositioned by passengers with alcohol on their breath, and had been through a few boyfriends.

Claire enjoyed showing me how to have a fun night out barhopping and meeting people, but she also liked lying around the apartment listening to me talk about literature. We were different in so many ways, but learned a lot from each other, and so far we seemed to work.

"I'm sleeping with a pilot but he's married so it's not going anywhere," she said over breakfast the first time she stayed over. When she saw I wasn't sure what to say to that, she added, "He doesn't know it yet, but his time is short."

I guess I had stolen some Delta pilot's girlfriend.

University life was foreign to her, and she was a little in awe of the rows of books that filled the walls of the grad student's apartment. She would hold Mr. Pink in her arms and stroke him while she browsed the bookshelves. "I can't imagine anybody having read all these," she said.

I told her he had probably read only parts of them. What I had learned in the great literature seminar was that the main thing was to know which books were really important, and to be familiar with the passages that made them so influential. Our prof said we were too busy with classes and social life to be expected to read complete books at our age. He said after graduation we were going to be unemployed and lying around on the couch at our parents' houses, and then we could revisit this literature at leisure.

Claire was properly impressed, as I hoped she would be, as she flipped through the first volume of Russell and Whitehead's *Principia Mathematica* with curiosity. "That's an important book nobody reads," I said. "They proved logic and mathematics are the same." I had taken freshman philosophy and knew enough to interpret one of the logical statements for her, but she had had enough and slipped it back on the shelf.

I assured her I was much more impressed with her

experiences as a world citizen than she ought to be with a book. "Then we should get married," she said. "Spouses of Delta employees can fly anywhere for practically nothing."

I had no idea how she intended that. "I should marry you so I can fly for free?"

"It doesn't mean anything," she said with the hint of a dismissive shrug. She was looking at *Portrait of the Artist as a Young Man.*"And we could go anywhere together."

"Claire, are you asking me to marry you?"

"We'll see." The faint trace of a smile flickered briefly across her face as she put the book back in place.

She wanted to see where I had grown up in Beaumont and meet my family, but I persuaded her to hold off on that until Thanksgiving. My mom would think I had stayed in Oklahoma for the summer because of a girl, which wasn't at all true, but I saw no need to stir that pot. Since Claire liked bars, I promised over Thanksgiving I'd show her so-called Fort Griffin, where Houston tavern owner Dick Dowling with just three cannon and about eighty men had stopped a Union ironclad invasion up the Sabine river to capture Beaumont. She always spent Christmas in Long Beach with her family, and said if I wanted to come that year she'd teach me how to surf.

I drove Claire to Will Rogers to put her on a shuttle to Dallas, and promised to look at a few apartments for us while she was gone. I was still trying to figure out how seriously I should take her casual remark about marriage. It occurred to me if we did that so we could go places together, but then it worked out, we could just stay married.

It was the end of August, and I was looking forward to the fall and to Thanksgiving and Christmas with Claire.

"Oh," she said as we kissed our goodbyes. "I almost forgot. I heard from Annie. Her parents found a really good house in Atlanta with a paddock. She might want to buy Posey back."

I had not seen it coming.

"Why would she want to do that?" I said. "I mean, she doesn't live at home anymore."

"I don't know," Claire said. "Anyway she's thinking about it. Can you find out who bought her?"

"I was just a volunteer and only worked a few days," I said. "They let me go because they couldn't take any more horses."

"There must be someone you can ask."

"Not really," I said. "The person who recruited me was a volunteer too." Somehow I had allowed myself to forget about Steve Willit, and wished she would drop this.

"Annie says Milton's Meadows is out of business. Something about a lawsuit."

"There's a lot of horses out there right now," I said. "She can have her pick and give one a nice home."

"No, she wants Posey." She kissed me goodbye. "Anyway, she said to ask. I'll tell her what you said." She kissed me again and disappeared into the terminal.

— iv —

The last time I saw Claire was at Laurel Tavern in Dallas. She didn't want to meet me again at all, but I wouldn't have it any other way. She agreed only reluctantly.

Two days earlier she had phoned out of the blue.

"Annie says Milton's Meadows was owned by Dominic Henstill, a registered kill buyer for a Mexican slaughterhouse company," she said. "He was paying commissions to volunteers for soliciting donated horses. What did you know about this, Leslie?"

There was a long silence. I grappled for words.

"Claire, I swear to God I can explain, but we have to meet somewhere to talk, because it's complicated."

She did not say anything.

"I don't want to lose you," I said. I was pleading now.

The night shuttle was half-empty, and the lights of Dallas that had once thrilled this Beaumont kid now seemed hollow on final approach. I had been running through my mind the things I was going to say. Somehow I had got it in my head that if I could only explain this right, she would understand. I would tell her about sub-par home mortgages and default rates and banks losing liquidity, and how there was not refuge space for ten percent of the excess horses on the market. She would see how it was a good thing to tell people the things they needed to hear when they had to let go of animals they could not afford.

The moment the plane touched down and began its

abrupt deceleration, a sinking realization swept over me. She was too well-traveled for such talk, and it would make no sense to her at all. Though I still could find no flaw in how Steve had explained these things, I knew what he said would simply not interest Claire.

She was already seated at the table when I showed up at Laurel Tavern. She looked devastated and hopeless. Three days ago it would have been unimaginable to me that I would see this self-assured girl in such a state. I took a seat but she did not say anything.

"Hi," I said, as gently as I could.

She looked up at me with moist and vulnerable eyes, waiting for me to say something magical to make all this go away.

"I only did it once," I said. "Annie was the only one, I swear. The minute I got home, I called my recruiter and quit."

"I don't want to be here," she said softly.

"Claire, please don't do this," I said. "I'm not ready to let you go. I wouldn't even know how to begin to do that. I don't want us to end."

"I don't hate you, Leslie," she said. "I thought I knew you, but I have no clue who you are or what you're about. I used to think I could read people, but I never even saw you coming. That's a new trick life played on me. I hadn't seen that one before."

"We can get past this," I said. "There's more to me than this. I can show you, but you have to give me the chance."

"I don't think I'd like that," she said. "I'm afraid of what I might find out and that scares me. It scares me a lot."

"Tell me what to do," I said. I was in despair. "Please, Claire. I'll do whatever you want."

"I need you to let me go," she said. "Promise you won't call, ever again. If you have any feelings at all for me, you have to promise that."

I believe Claire meant it when she said she didn't hate me. But she was stranded on the far side of a river of my own creation, one without bridges or fords, and too wide and deep for either of us to cross.

It was the hardest thing I ever did, when I agreed to respect her wishes.

I stay away from her every day now. It's the first thing I do when I wake up in the morning. When I take a shower and brush my teeth, I'm staying away from Claire. When I'm studying for mid-terms, I'm staying away from Claire. If I'm watching TV, I'm staying away from Claire. If I pass finals next spring, I'll be a junior at OU who's staying away from Claire.

I still can't say whether Steve was right or wrong because I just can't tell about those things anymore. I wouldn't have lost Claire if I hadn't gotten involved with him, but I wouldn't have found her in the first place either. I wish we could have met some other way, but I don't see how else on earth our paths would have ever crossed if I hadn't shown up to talk Annie Holm out of her horse.

Claire's last words linger in my head like it was yesterday. When she got up from the table to leave, she said, "Leslie, this is going to hurt for a long, long time."

GRANDPA GOES
TO MEXICO

Somebody cracked Wesley Boyd in the back of the head with a pool stick and dropped him like a rock. One minute he was lining up a shot, and the next he was face-down on the barroom floor, whiffing stale tobacco and rancid beer in the sawdust. His mind went missing in a low ground fog trying to figure out what in batshit hell had just happened. He must have got into an argument with somebody while shooting pool. Then when he leaned in for his shot, the bastard clipped him from behind with the butt end of a stick. For the life of him, he could not put a finger on who had done it or what they had been arguing about.

Lying very still with his eyes shut, Wes gradually became aware that he did not hurt anywhere. He felt good enough to jump to his feet and surprise the son of a bitch, and punch his lights out. He decided to do that. But when he went to make his move, he suddenly felt bad all over like he had tumbled down several flights of stairs. He decided to rest another minute. About then he noticed everything had gone very quiet. The bartender must have thrown him out into the street while he was passed out, so he could lock up the place and go home.

Wes rolled onto his side, and discovered the ground was neither hard like street dirt nor firm like a barroom floor. It was soft and rustled when he moved. This made no sense. It was as if he was face-down in a thick bed of leaves that had broken his fall. Maybe he had not been out drinking after all, and had not gotten into a fight while shooting pool.

He must have been riding Selznick in search of a calf that had gone missing from pasture, and hit his head on a tree branch. His head was probably bleeding, but the leaves had saved him from serious injury. It was a relief to know that he was not going to have a hangover, and would not have to explain to Sophie where he had been all night. He opened his eyes to see if he was right. It was daylight sure enough, but starting to get dark, which meant he had been down several hours. Sophie and the kids would be frantic with worry, and he did not want them out looking for him at night. Selznick could not have wandered far. He would get to his feet and find him, and ride back to the house and call it a day.

He decided to do that. It felt so good on the soft leaves that he lingered a moment. But then he shouted, "Okay Wes, enough of this nonsense! Let's go home."

He threw off a blanket, and to his surprise saw that he was not resting on a carpet of leaves under a tree out in pasture as he had imagined. He had been tucked away in somebody's bed, in a bedroom he did not recognize, and it was not evening falling but dawn that was breaking outside the window.

Wes sat up and tried to make sense of this. He had not fallen off a horse, nor had he been in a bar fight. The reason he felt all busted up was because he was ninety-seven years old. He woke up feeling like this every morning, but it had slipped his mind during the night.

He still did not understand whose bedroom he had slept in, or why his wife was not there with him. It was not the bedroom on the ranch where he and Sophie had lived for many years and raised seven children. This must be sometime after they retired and sold the place. They moved to the little town of Shiner, Texas, where she had grown up, and bought a house where they lived many years. Those had been good days.

Back when he was ranching Wes would rise at four a.m., fix a cup of coffee in the kitchen, and listen to the farm and ranch agriculture reports on AM radio. After they retired to Shiner he no longer had to get up so early, but it was ingrained in him to start the day with AM farm and ranch reports. He moved the radio from the kitchen so he could listen to it in bed. Though such things no longer mattered, he would follow cattle, sow belly, and grain prices on the Chicago Exchange, updates on inches of rainfall for the year, and the weather forecast for the day. Sophie did not complain about him turning on the radio at four a.m. but began sleeping in the other bedroom.

During the day he always had some project or other that kept him out from under her feet. He had started a little garden in the backyard where he mostly grew tomatoes that he was very proud of and would share with the neighbors. They brought the barometer and rain gauge from the ranch, and he now used them to keep a written log of daily temperature and rainfall, though it served no purpose. Sophie mostly spent her time visiting neighbors, or shopping for groceries and other needs in town. They both looked forward to visits from the children and grandchildren.

Though Wes remembered those days of retirement fondly, he knew that he was not in the Shiner house bedroom, either. It came to him that Sophie had died two or three years back. The children and grandchildren would not allow him to live alone in Shiner after that. His grandchildren, who were grown with families of their own now, took turns putting him up for a few months at a time on their ranches. Some mornings he might wake up in Weatherford, and a couple months later in Mineral Wells, and then in Sealy or Brenham or Rosenberg.

It was his own fault that he was in this fix. They had been happy in Shiner where they were independent and lived as they pleased. One day Wes got fed up with telemarketers constantly calling to sell him everything from hearing aids and wheelchairs to gold and silver coins. He notified the phone company that he wanted his telephone removed because they did not need it. The children worried that he and Sophie would not be able to call for help in an emergency, and bought them a smartphone. Wes decided that it was too smart for him, but Sophie had learned how to use it.

One night Sophie came into his room and woke him because she was having difficulty breathing. She was in such distress that she could not use the smartphone. Wes had to pull on his pants and go outside to wake up one of the neighbors. It was the middle of the night, and he did not move so fast anymore, and he had to go to two or three houses before he finally woke somebody up. They called an ambulance that took Sophie to the hospital, but she passed away that same night.

Wes knew that the bedroom he woke up in this morning was not any of the ones he had been in before. It was modest but comfortable, and when a breeze stirred the curtains the country outside looked different too. This was not Weatherford or Sealy or any of those places. He was not in Texas anymore.

It seemed to him that his nephew's grandson, Matt, had married a Dallas girl named Josiane sometime back, and they had moved to California. He must be with them now. Sometimes it was hard to remember who he was staying with when he woke up, though such confusions usually sorted themselves out as the day went on.

Sitting in a strange bedroom at age ninety-seven, he wondered how in the world he had allowed himself to come to this. Back in younger days he used to look at old folks with a certain awe, and wonder why in the world they had allowed themselves to slip into such bad shape. He had resolved that he would never permit that to happen to him. When he had met Sophie, he could not imagine it happening to her, either. But she was gone from his life now, and would not be back. He did not like thinking about these things in an unfamiliar bedroom.

He slid back down into the bed and instead thought back to the days before he had set eyes on Sophie or had even known she existed. Once when he and Jimmy Salter were about twenty, they had, on a dare, set out on horseback to ford the Rio Grande and shoot pool in a bar in Mexico. A shy but achingly pretty young girl was cleaning tables there, and she could not take her eyes off him. Probably she didn't get to see many boys her age. He wanted in the worst way to say something to her, and maybe take her someplace nice. But he and Jimmy were both pretty thin financially, and he did not have the courage to talk to her. He resolved that he was going to save up some money over the summer and then return to court her. He was pretty sure she would like that. She had haunted him in memory for a long time, but somehow or other he never did make it back there to find her.

He had not thought of the girl for many years until

this morning. But it seemed like only yesterday that he and Jimmy had forded the Rio Grande to that little cantina. Once again he felt the girl's soft, dark eyes on him while they shot pool. It was all so real he believed the Rio Grande must surely be right outside the bedroom window where a breeze stirred the curtains. And not very far past that, the girl was still cleaning tables at the cantina.

When he lay very still in the bed and did not move, he did not feel any different than when he was twenty. He did not understand why he should not go outside and saddle up Selznick, and ford the river and find the girl. He was brave enough to court her now. Maybe that would be a good project for the day.

When he sat up and swung his feet to the floor, suddenly he was ninety-seven again. He considered this for a moment. It seemed to him that if he could feel twenty lying very still in bed, there was no reason why he could not feel the same age on his feet. The thing was to just do it, and to dismiss the rest as nonsense. Anyway, he had kept the girl waiting long enough.

Wes pulled on his pants and put on a shirt, and that went all right. There was a pair of boots in the closet that fit, and he pulled them on, too. He looked around the ranch house a little, and sure enough it was Matt and Josiane's place, but nobody else was home. Matt and the boys were on the road showing horses, and Josiane worked at the Valley Kitchen Cafe in town. She had fixed a breakfast for him, and it was still warm in the oven. He felt even more confident after eating it. Then he packed a saddlebag with some cold roast beef from the icebox and a pan of cornbread from the stove. By the time he walked to the barn with the saddlebag, he felt sure that he was close to twenty again. It was going to be all right.

He took a halter from a nail near the barn entrance, and went looking through the stalls for Selznick. Most of the horses were gone, but sure enough there was his chestnut gelding over in the fourth stall on the left.

"Hey, Selznick!" he said. "Guess what, lazy bones? Time to move your ass. We're going to Mexico!"

"Wrong chestnut, old man," the horse told him. "There's no Selznick in this barn."

Wes looked at him more closely. "Don't mess with me today, Selznick. We have places to go and things to do."

"Stick it, bud. I'm not him."

"You saying I don't know my own horse?"

"It's not my fault if you tied one on last night."

"You have a loose lip, chestnut. So who in the hell are you?"

"In the arena I'm Lightning Jack Prescott, but around the barn everybody just calls me Ralph."

"You must be a pretty piss poor cutter if they went on the road and left you in the barn."

"I'm all right on a good day, but I won't load in a trailer. Matt says it's not worth it. He says he'll settle for a 72 on another horse before he'll try to load me for a 74."

"I could have you in a trailer in one minute flat."

"You're in for a big surprise if you believe that."

Wes was not accustomed to such sass from a horse, but admired his spunk. He looked the animal over, taking his measure. "Ralph, let me ask you a question. You ever been to Mexico?"

"I've been around. Nevada, Arizona, Texas, Oklahoma, those places. The usual circuit. Can't say I've been to Mexico."

"How'd you like go down there with me?"

"When, now?"

"Sure. We'll see a little of the country."

"What for?"

"Well, I have a girl there who's sweet on me. Works in a cantina. I intend to court her today. It's not very far, and you won't need to load in a trailer."

Ralph mulled this over. "I've got news for you. You can't get to Mexico from here."

"It's just across the river."

"I don't know where you've been, but a lot has happened while you were gone. They paved over the main trail to Mexico a long time ago. It's an interstate now, and horses aren't allowed there. I suppose we could take the San Marcos pass, but that goes into Santa Barbara. It's all urban development down there now, and zoning laws don't permit me to trespass."

The old man shook his head. "Ralph, you have to be the most mixed-up gelding I ever saw. Stick with me and you'll learn something."

He slipped on the halter and led Ralph around to the tack room, where he found a saddle and blanket. Back in the day Wes could toss a saddle with ease, but on this morning he struggled to drag one outside to his horse. He borrowed the chair that propped open the tack room door and placed the saddle on that. From there he was able to sling it up onto the gelding.

"That cinch isn't nearly tight enough," Ralph told him.

It was as tight as the old man could pull it. "Did I ask your advice? I was doing this long before you were born," he said.

Wes climbed unsteadily onto the chair, grabbed the saddle horn, and with a foot in the stirrup was able to pull himself on board. The cinch was not secure, and the saddle slipped a little askew by the time Wes settled into it. He tested the balance, and it seemed to him good enough to ride, so they set out for Mexico.

The old man noticed that West Texas had changed a lot since the last time he had passed through this part. Back when he and Jimmy were cowhands for some outfit, the country had been a flat treeless prairie. Now the land was buckled up with hills so that it resembled a crumpled blanket, and cottonwoods and oak groves had sprouted up to dot the landscape. They passed through the sleepy little town of Buellton that had not been there before. It seemed like a nice enough place, and he did not understand how they could have missed it. He stopped at the cemetery to see if he knew anybody buried there, but the names were unfamiliar, so they moved on.

Somewhere around four that afternoon they arrived at the river. The water was low and slow, winding peacefully through the chaparral along its banks. There was a high ridge on the far side that he did not recognize, and Wes figured he must have miscalculated by a couple of miles. But the river was unmistakable.

"Well, chestnut," he said with a gesture of his hand. "I give you the Rio Grande."

"You must have hit your head when you fell out of bed this morning," Ralph said. "That's the Santa Ynez. I come out here a lot, so I ought to know."

"Horse, you talk a good game," Wes replied. "But that don't make you an expert. What you see over on the far side is Mexico. I'm about to court a pretty girl who works in a cantina not far from here."

Wes moved the horse forward into the shallow stream, and they forded easily, leaving a wedge of ripples on the glassy surface in their wake. There was lush pasture on the opposite bank, though it shortly gave way to yet more chaparral which ran all the way up the foothills. They emerged from the river and he spun the gelding around for a look at this beautiful country.

"Okay, Ralph, now you can tell the barn you've been to Mexico!"

"I'll keep this our little secret."

Wes studied the high ridgeline that had not been there years before. "We need to follow that thing and find a pass somewhere."

"I'm not going anywhere near the interstate," Ralph told him. "There's the San Marcos pass, but it's quite a ways yet."

The sun was low in the sky and there was a slight chill in the air, so Wes slid from the saddle. "This is far enough for one day," he said. "We'll get started again at first light."

He removed his sleeping bag and unbridled Ralph. The saddle had slid even further at a cocked angle because it was not tightly cinched, but Wes decided not to remove it. He was not sure he could get it back on Ralph again without the chair from the tack room. "There's plenty of water and good grazing out here," he said. "You can go look after yourself."

Wes was too tired to build a campfire. He ate the cold roast beef with cornbread while Ralph grazed along the river. After sundown the stars came out with a quarter moon in the west, and blessed them with a peaceful night. Wes snuggled in his sleeping bag and looked up at the moon and contemplated the pretty girl at the cantina who was sweet on him. When he saw her tomorrow, he intended to apologize for having taken so long to return for her. He felt bad about that but was confident she would forgive him.

Ralph thoroughly enjoyed the clean night air, fresh

water, and sweet grassland. Wes nestled under an oak tree in his sleeping bag and had the best night's sleep he had known in a long time.

The morning sun broke behind the ridgeline, and he slept late in the shade of the ridge. When he woke, he allowed himself to lie and watch Ralph grazing near the river. Wes was always in his twenties or thirties when he dreamed, and if he lay very still, he would feel that way after he woke up. He figured the cantina could not be more than three or four miles on the other side of the ridge. They ought to make it by noon or so.

He had begun to doze off again thinking of the girl, when he heard the sound of a horse splashing across the river toward them. Someone, a boy, shouted at them in Spanish.

"Papa Boyd! Hello! Is that you?"

It was some Mexican kid of about ten, barefoot and wearing only jeans, bareback on a spotted appaloosa. His horse sprang from the river and approached. Wes sat up as the kid looked down at him. The boy looked familiar, but Wes could not put a finger on where he had seen him before.

The boy again shouted across the river. *"Josiane! I have found him! He is here!"* He waited a moment, but there was no response. Whoever he was calling did not hear him.

"What's wrong, son?" Wes asked. "Are you in trouble?"

"Papa Boyd, they have called the sheriff. Everyone is trying to

find you. Josiane, she is not happy." He turned and shouted once again. *"Josiane! Over here!"*

Still no reply. He looked at Wes's horse and shook his head. *"Ralph, you are in so much trouble. Big time!"* The boy turned the appaloosa and splashed back across the river, returning the way he had come.

"Oh sure. Blame it on me," Ralph said. "Tell me I didn't see that coming."

"Well, horse face," Wes said with a chuckle. "Let me ask you a question. Did that kid look like a Mexican to you? What country do you suppose we're in now?" Ralph did not deign to reply.

"Anyway," Wes added,"my Spanish is a little rusty. What did he want?"

"That was Juan David, the trainer's son. He works for your nephew's grandson Matt. And for Matt's wife, Josiane."

"I know who Josiane is," Wes said, pulling on his pants. "She's that Sealy girl."

"No, you're thinking of Brin Spacek. The one your cousin Edwin married. You stayed with them in Brenham before you came to California."

Wes frowned. "I didn't know Brin was a Spacek. I thought she was Alan Foster's little girl."

"That's Danielle. She's married to Robert."

"Oh, that's right."

"Anyway, Josiane is from Dallas. She married your nephew's grandson, Matt. They've been putting you up out here in California."

Wes thought about that a moment. "Josiane … is she one of those Sadler girls?"

"That I don't know. She might be a Sadler, but I couldn't say for sure." Ralph thought a moment. "Now, your cousin Earl, he married a Sadler."

"I don't have a cousin Earl."

"Sure, you do. He's your second cousin on your wife's side."

"Oh, that's right. I forgot about him."

"I don't recall if any of the Boyds married a Sadler. Sophie would know, but she's dead now."

Wes was on his feet and pulling up his pants and looking for his shirt.

"Sophie Wallenski, now there was a beautiful woman," he said. "Her papa sure didn't have much use for me, I'll tell you that. But Sophie, God bless her, knew what she wanted. For about a year after we married, her old man would flush beet red in the face anytime I walked into the room. He got over it eventually. I was always grateful to her for that. I sure was crazy about that girl. Yes sir, treated her right, too. A few things about me aggravated her sometimes, and she had some funny habits I had to put up with. But overall we got along real good. I have to say that we did."

Two riders splashed into the river from the far bank and moved toward them. One was Juan David on the appaloosa. The other a straw-blonde woman in her thirties riding a sorrel.

"Oh boy, here comes Josiane," Ralph sighed. "She's not bringing any apples, either."

Wes struggled to zip up his pants as Josiane pulled up to him on the sorrel. She was furious beyond words. "Grandpa Boyd, what is the matter with you!" she shrieked. "The sheriff's department and everybody is out looking for you! What do you think you're doing?"

Wes looked up at her. "Are you one of those Sadler girls?"

"Damn straight I'm a Sadler, I'm the one married to Matt. Now you talk to me, Grandpa! Do you know the sheriff organized a search party on account of you?"

"Go tell him to jump to hell. I can look out for myself. Anyway I don't want people looking for me."

"I'm responsible for you while the boys are on the road! I had to call Matt in Oklahoma and tell him what happened. He's waiting to hear from me. They're planning to cancel their trip to come help find you."

"He in Oklahoma City?"

"Yes, and he made the finals. It's important to him!"

"How'd they do at Will Rogers?"

"Fourth with a 213. Oh, don't even ask me that! Why would you care? You don't care about anybody but yourself." She took out her smartphone and called her husband. "Matt? He's out here by the river and he's fine. Yes, Juan David found him. I don't know, he just went off with Ralph somewhere. They spent the night out here." She tried to hand the phone to Wes. "Matt wants to talk to you."

"Tell him I said he's too piss poor of a cutter to waste my time. I want him to take Oklahoma with at least a 220. Then we'll talk."

She spoke with Matt a little longer and hung up. "My God, you are such a mess, Grandpa! Don't you know people love you? We go crazy with worry when you do stuff like this! Why do you put us through this?"

"I got business to take care of."

"What's that supposed to mean?"

Wes hesitated in a moment of embarrassment, then mumbled quickly, "I'm going to see my girlfriend."

Josiane was a little taken aback, but recovered. "Your …? Oh, okay. Which one are you talking about?"

"You don't know her. It was a long time ago, back when me and Jimmy Salter went down to Mexico. She's real pretty, a little shy, works in a cantina. Had her eye on me the whole time. She likes me, I can tell you that."

"Where in Mexico? And who's Jimmy Salter?"

"Jimmy passed away, he was before your time. But it's not far from here. Little bit above Laredo. We need to figure out how to get past this ridge somehow."

Bewildered, Josiane softened a little. "Does Sophie know you have a girlfriend?"

"I haven't met Sophie yet. See, she won't find out because it's before her time. That's not cheating, is it?"

Josiane looked at him. "No," she said gently, "I don't suppose it's cheating."

"I'm glad you think so. I was a little worried about that part."

"Listen to me, Grandpa. Matt says you can't go to Mexico today because he needs you at the ranch. He wants you to help me look after things while they're hauling. Can you do that for us?"

Wes quietly scuffled his boots. "Sure, I suppose I can put this off for Matt. Anyway I've pretty much figured out how to get there now. Few more days won't make much difference."

"Juan David, will you gather up Grandpa's saddlebag and things and bring them?"

"Yes, ma'am."

Josiane fetched Ralph, and saw the saddle resting at a crooked angle on him. "Oh, my God in heaven! Grandpa, did you loosen this cinch or were you riding him this way?"

Wes looked at the saddle, but he could not remember and did not answer.

"You could have been killed!" She sighed. "You know what? I'm going to have to hide your clothes in a drawer someplace so you can't leave the house without telling somebody." She tightened the cinch, and helped Wes up into the saddle.

"Juan, I want you to know that your daddy and everybody else are going to be real proud of you for finding Grandpa," she said to the boy. "Sheriff Dexter might even give you a reward. You were a real hero today."

Juan grinned. "Yes, ma'am!"

"And Ralph," she said, turning to him.

"Oh, boy. Here it comes," Ralph said.

"You have been a bad horse. Bad, bad, bad! Don't you dare run off with Grandpa like that ever again. You scared the life out of us. No apples for you for a week!"

"Don't pay any attention to her, Ralph," Wes said. "The ladies will act pretty mean sometimes, but they never can make it stick with a horse. She'll bring you an apple in a day or two."

"Grandpa, you stay out of this!" she said.

The three of them set out across the river for home.

Matt stayed on the road and took Oklahoma City with a 221. Wes wanted to hear all about it, and Matt told him over the phone.

Ralph liked to work cows in the arena, but did not miss the part about traveling halfway to hell across country in trailers all summer. Josiane put him out to pasture so he could graze at inclination or just stand in the shade of a tree and contemplate life. Sure enough, the very next day, she brought him an apple just as Wes had predicted.

The adventure with the old man had been a new experience for Ralph. It was a welcome break from his daily routine; he got to see a little of the country and experience life on the far side of the river. He would not have minded if Grandpa Boyd took him out to explore again sometime.

But that was not going to happen anytime soon. Josiane had taken away all of Grandpa's pants and hidden them in her bedroom closet.

LOST HORSES

"I'll bet you don't know what that is," the old man said.

"Sure I do," I told him, setting my foot on it and pushing at it to see if it would move. It did not. "It's a watering trough for horses," I said. The gray box looked a little like a concrete bathtub, but was on the small side for a grown man. It was dry as a bone.

The old fellow studied me for a moment and nodded. He had not expected somebody my age could identify it. "Usually I can tell people it's most anything and they believe it."

"Probably there used to be a hitching post right about here," I said, holding two hands in the air to show him. "Once you watered your horse, you could hitch him up and go inside to shop or shoot pool, or whatever else you've got in that store."

"My hitching post went to rot and fell apart a long time ago," he said. "I didn't see the sense to replacing it since nobody ever used it. I keep the drain open in the trough, too. Otherwise after a rain we have a mosquito problem."

"A few small towns still have troughs like this," I said. "The ones I've seen they've mostly turned into planters."

"Turned them into what?"

"Well, they fill them with dirt and plant flowers in them. It's real pretty. You ought to think about it."

He did, for about a second. "I'm not going to do something like that."

"Why not?"

"People would think I'm an idiot."

We were somewhere deep in the Big Thicket north of Beaumont, which is mostly a mixture of pastureland and dense piney woods forest. Much of it is swampland in a season of average rainfall but had dried out after several years of drought. The old man was tipped back in a chair against the wall of a weathered and paint-peeled general store located on a gravel crossroads. I supposed him to be on the lookout for customers. My grandfather's pickup parked down the road was the only hint of a prospect in sight. But the pickup was not in need of water and did not require a hitching post to prevent it from wandering off.

"How old are you, son?"

"Eighteen."

"Do you work or go to school?"

"Well, actually I just graduated. I'm going to college at Austin in the fall."

"What's your name?"

"Larry Malik."

"I don't know any Maliks around here."

"No, we drove up from Houston for the day. My grandfather is visiting an old friend down the road there. You might know him. T.J. Harvey."

"I know T.J. very well."

"Grandpa worked for him back in the nineteen-fifties. T.J. was crew chief on a doodlebug crew. They blew shot lines all over out here for one of the big oil companies."

"Yes, I remember when T.J. was doing that."

"I came out here with Grandpa today because I wanted to see a little of the Big Thicket."

"What do you think of it?"

"Well, it's not as wet as I expected."

"We're in a drought right now."

"Grandpa said back when he was working for T.J., he had to wade through ten or fifteen yards of swamp with a cable and then wrap it around a pine tree. The drill truck would reel in the cable to pull itself up to the tree. They got through the swamp from one tree to the next like that."

"They used to eat lunch here at my store sometimes," the old man said.

I decided to impress him a little more with how much I knew of country life. "Another thing I can tell you about hitching up horses," I said. "If you're going to be gone for a while, you ought to switch him to a halter. He'll be a lot more comfortable without the bit." I was a little proud of myself for knowing that.

"And how would a fellow do that?" he asked. "Do you mean he has to take a halter with him every time he leaves the house?"

I hadn't thought about that. I'd seen a lot of movies where cowboys rode up to a cantina, tethered their horses to the hitching post, and went inside to drink and play cards. I could not recall any in which they took the time to switch their horses from bridles to halters.

"I couldn't really say," I admitted. "Probably on manhunts and long trips they had to take halters along." I was guessing.

"Have you ever even been on a horse?"

"Sure," I said.

"What kind do you have?"

"I don't actually own one. But I've been on horseback rides."

"Do you get along with them?"

"Well, they don't seem to mind me. Horses don't take to you as easily as a dog. The ones I rode didn't seem to particularly care about me one way or another. Stable horses mostly just want to go home."

"You ought to save up some money and buy yourself a horse. There's plenty of boarding ranches around Houston where you could keep him."

"What would I want to do that for?"

"You learn a lot from a horse that you won't find out any other way. They may be a lot of trouble to look after, but you won't find a better friend."

"If I had money, I sure wouldn't spend it on a horse."

"What would you buy?"

"I'd get a car so I could date girls."

"You can use your folks' car for that."

"Mom always needs it for something or other. Pop has a pickup he uses for a little grocery store we own on a strip mall. But I wouldn't want to take a girl out in that."

"If a girl is interested in you, she won't care if you have a car. I didn't have one when I met my wife. It might impress her if you owned a horse."

"Maybe out here. It's different in Houston. Girls expect you to take them places. I know one from school that I like a lot and I'm pretty sure she likes me. I'd ask her out, but Mom doesn't want me taking girls on dates in her car."

The old man shook his head. "Young people have lost interest in horses. There was a time when the horse was a part of the family. He worked your cattle, took you to places you needed to be, and I guarantee he was your best friend in good times and bad."

"It might have been like that once. You're not up to date with modern times."

"That's what I'm talking about with you kids today," he said. "Of course you don't want to groom a horse or muck out a stall. But you'll crawl under a damn automobile and pull out the transmission in a heartbeat. You won't blink at overhauling the engine. Some kids even give their cars names, like it was a horse or something."

"If I had a car I'd probably give it a name."

I could see the old fellow was getting fed up with me. I didn't intend to make him mad exactly, but did feel I needed to bring him up to date. I placed my foot on the water trough and pushed at it again. "You ought to pull this thing out of the ground," I said, "and store it out back somewhere if you're so headstrong on keeping it. Nobody needs it anymore. When people drive up to your store, they have to walk around this thing to get inside. One of these days somebody is going to hurt themselves, and then you're going to have a whopping big lawsuit on your hands."

"That trough is doing fine right where it is," he said. "It's been there over a century and hasn't hurt anybody yet. I feel sorry for somebody who can't walk around a horse trough without skinning his shins or getting busted up."

"When was the last time anyone watered a horse here? You don't even have any water in there, anymore."

"I can put water in it anytime I want. Somebody might need it one day."

He was getting a little testy. I stood my ground.

"Nobody is going to need this thing ever again," I said. "I don't understand why you want to keep it out here where somebody can get hurt on it."

"I'll tell you why and then you'll know," he said. "I believe the horse is going to make a comeback someday."

I couldn't believe what I was hearing. "Why would you think that?"

"The horse has been around for thousands of years," he said. "People only switched to the car in the last hundred years or so."

"They switched to the car because it's better." I was starting to think he really was an old fool. "Maybe we didn't have cars for thousands of years, but we've got them now. Nobody wants horses anymore."

"I believe people are getting fed up with cars," he said. "I see people kick and swear at them all the time."

"Somebody might kick his tires when he's mad," I said. "But I've never seen anybody trade one in for a horse."

"They will when the oil is gone," he said, looking me in the eye.

"What are you talking about now?"

"It's in the news all the time. Scientists predict the world is going to run out of oil."

"That's not going to happen tomorrow."

"I didn't say tomorrow. But look at how many people you see driving around in cars like idiots. They're burning up all the oil. Pretty soon there won't be any left."

I tried to think of an answer to that. "The government wouldn't allow that to happen," I said.

"The government won't be able to do anything about it," he said. "You'll have to figure out some other way to date girls when the oil is gone."

"Scientists will come up with something."

"I believe scientists will rediscover the horse. It is still the best friend man ever had. People might have forgotten about him, but he hasn't forgotten us. Horses know the internal combustion engine is a fly-by-night fad. Go watch them graze in a pasture. Do they look worried to you? They're biding their time, waiting for the oil to run out. They know once that happens we'll come running back to them. We're going to be like the fellow who tried to borrow money from his ex-wife. They'll be a little uppity at first, but they'll come around once they see how much we need them."

I had to shake my head because I was pretty much done arguing. Anyway I'd run out of ideas and couldn't think of anything else to say that might turn his head around.

"Once the oil is gone, you're going to see people scramble to find water troughs and hitching posts for horses again. I'll sit out here in this chair and laugh because I'll have the jump on them. You might think I'm a fool, but I believe the time is coming. I might be too old, but you'll see it in your lifetime."

I gave up and walked back to T.J.'s house, where my grandfather and I had lunch with him and his wife.

We started back to Houston in Grandpa's pickup in late afternoon. We had to make our way along a narrow dirt road through piney woods to reach the connection to the Beaumont highway. After a few miles the forest gave way to a stretch of open pasture. I spotted a couple of brown horses grazing out there. Their ears popped forward and they looked up when they heard us coming. They followed us with their eyes and I looked at them as we drove past. When I glanced back at them, they were grazing again.

It occurred to me they might have looked up to see if we had run out of oil yet. Once they saw we had not, they lost interest and returned to grazing. They seemed lazy and content, as if they had all the time in the world.

ABOUT THE AUTHOR

Mark Saha grew up in cotton country along the Texas Gulf Coast, earned a BA at the University of Notre Dame, and attended film school at UCLA, where a collection of his short stories won a Samuel Goldwyn Creative Writing Award and led to many years of writing scripts for film and television. Growing up in Texas he worked on a doodlebug crew blowing shot lines across the Big Thicket, drove a tractor hauling trash wagons at a cotton gin near Fairchild, and worked cattle on foot on his father's farm outside Sealy. He lives in Santa Monica, California.

Made in United States
North Haven, CT
23 January 2023

31473496R00096